The
Passion of Bright Young
Things

Rohan

For Kate

THURSDAY

'What news have you darling, of the outside world?'

'What do you suspect has changed so much in the hour you have been in class?'

'Hopefully much.'

'Not in an hour, no.'

'Shame really.'

'Can't people hear you typing on your laptop?'

'I imagine so. But maybe I'm just taking notes?'

'Taking notes on what today?'

'Dr Huxley's third presentation this semester on German Expressionist Art and Hardcore Pornography. Also, German.'

'Is that not all a bit much for a Thursday morning?'

'Well, I mean this is rather light compared to most of his lectures. Before he got stuck on this, it was *Incest and Surrealism*. Not German.'

'I think we might have covered that in the third year of that degree when I was doing it. Not the first.'

'It appears the curriculum has changed somewhat since your time at The College of Fine Arts darling. All those years ago.'

'Last year?'

'Precisely.'

'They're just taking longer to get to the good bits by the sounds of it. Ok well, carry on then. Where were we?'

'Yes, the boy. Well he had one of those un-retractable foreskins, you see. You know when the opening is too tight to be pulled over the head of the cock and the whole thing just sits there like the mouth of some hairless, angry looking rodent?'

'I don't, but goodness me. How complicated.'

'Obviously it's not the worst sex I've had. And clearly not the worst you would have had either. Good length though, good girth too thing thing. He seemed to know how to use it in the end. I was playing along though. Making all the usual noises. Rolling about, making my eyes flick back into my skull like that rodent's mouth was hitting my prostate directly. Over and over again. But my mind was elsewhere. All I kept thinking was, How in the world was he able to clean it?'

'What?'

'The Rodent. There I am, face down in the bed, a hand on either ass cheek, pretending to be pleasured to the point of hallucination. My skull pounding against that awful headboard. You know the one, with quilted crushed blue velvet?'

'Yes. Vile.'

'… and all I can think is, So what does he do to clean it? How does he clean the Rodent? Then my mind starts going to places like, Well maybe he cleans it with a cue tip dipped in some Dettol. Just like, swishes it around inside or something?'

'I don't think that would work as well as you seem to think.'

'This foreskin business can be rather complicated can't it? Not that I have a preference either way. I mean, it's not supposed to be complicated. We seem to cope just fine, don't we? Well I mean, I do. Christ knows about that thing between your legs. Probably not seen the light of day since September 11.'

'And equally yours I'm certain probably hasn't seen a day's rest since September 11.'

'Internet dating is all very convenient, but it just seems a bit flawed. I made sure, like you said, to ask for multiple pictures, from multiple angles but still, what do I get stuck with? An excess of unretractable foreskin preventing any real kind of genuine interaction with what lies beneath.'

'What website were you using this time?'

'Manhunt.com this week. Seems to be the latest thing. The colour scheme is awful though. This horrible, kind of American Frat-House blue and yellow everywhere with little tanned, headless torsos peppered all over the screen and inarticulate messages popping up every two minutes.
Hey, how r u? U up? Wots doing? I mean, I know they're missing a head, but I still do insist on some degree of grammar or eloquence.'

'Messages popping up every two minutes? That's rich.'

'Honestly! Men become very forthcoming when they know you can't see who they really are.'

'Well, I assume most people in general…'

'Asking all sorts of vile, interesting things. Rim jobs, piss play, anal stretching. And that was all before midnight. On a Wednesday!'

'One's sexual desires don't abide by the confines of school-night etiquette.'

'Yes, but if they're being asked to be pissed on at 9:30pm on a Wednesday, what could they possibly be up to on a fucking Saturday?'

'I think it's best not to concern yourself with it.'

'Seems like it's the glory hole of the 21st Century though, this cruising for sex online, doesn't it? Computers now are that small, dark void that men are able to discreetly shove themselves through, fuck till their hearts content and then go back to their normal lives and wives and children, their Dalmatians and their BMW's and try their best to forget it ever happened. It's all very anonymous.'

'Until it's not.'

'Yes, until it's not and they need to see you. Until they can't bear the chat room banter any longer and must smash through that dark, illuminated monitor glass. That wall, that perfect mechanism for preventing them seeing what they know in their hearts is true but what their minds can't seem to comprehend. That on the other side of that wall, there is another man about to be latched onto their cock. The monitor, that glory hole is now just the beginning though. And what they shove through is a small thumbnail picture of their chest, dick, ass, a discreet side profile. A discreet, naked outline of some shoulders in the shadows. Discreet. Always discreet. God forbid someone ever advertised themselves as indiscreet on these things. 23 years old, tall, swimmers build, open, loud, and will broadcast the intimate details of the impending tryst with any and all who will listen. Also, no gag reflex.'

'No that's long gone I imagine.'

'What is it these men think we owe them to maintain such discretion? A complete stranger, lurking around our house, freshly released from their natural habitat of suburban fencing and primary school runs, requesting we now burden ourselves with their most intimate of secrets. Are you discreet? Yes. I am. But I won't be about this.'

'So, just a few questions so far…'

'Of course.'

'Swimmers build? Is that what we're saying now?'

'I swim.'

'Well I'm not doubting you know how to swim darling but having a swimmers build is certainly another thing in itself entirely. I can drive, but I'm not putting Formula 1 down as a hobby, am I?'

'I feel my body, reflects that of which a swimmer would naturally be defined after a lifetime of swimming. It's long, it's lean. I have large hands.'

'You can go for long periods of time having your breathing restricted.'

'Listen. There are only four boxes to tick, ok? Thin, Swimmers, Muscled and Heavy. This site doesn't necessarily lend itself to going into deep, physiological descriptions about how you came, in your early 20s, to be the size and shape you are right now.'

'Four boxes huh? That's all we get?'

'Yes. You are either skinny, skinny but with definition, a gym junkie or fat.'

'Hmmm. It's almost like those charts you see showing the evolution of humans from being hunched over chimps to fully erect walking people, isn't it? We start as skinny young boys, we grow, get lean, then as our looks start to fade, we overcompensate at the gym and then finally as our bodies shut down and we get fat.'

'The evolution of the faggot.'

'Something like that, yes.'

'So is there room to explain your build to others, in further detail later? I feel like you might need some clarification here."

'Yes, I assume you can if you feel the need to. But there are other boxes as well which are meant to say more about you.'

'How many more.'

'Just four.'

'So, eight boxes in total?'

'Yes. Twink. Jock. Bear and Daddy.'

'Ah, yes, that's much clearer now.'

'It's all very efficient. And there's filters too. So, no need to bother with anything you're not feeling up to that night.'

'So, the Slim Bears and the Swimming Jocks can have a rest and we just focus on the Fat Daddies for tonight?'

'Correct.'

'I'm not entirely sure where I sit in all that though.'

'What does it matter? Just play along to get your cheap thrills and go back to whatever sub-cultural fence it was you were sitting on before you logged on. So anyway, this foreskin…'

'Yes, sorry. Carry on…'

'He rolls off me after it's all finished, and I get up to tidy myself. But once it's become obvious it's his cue to leave, you know that thing I do with the lull in conversation and then the sigh?'

'Sadly, yes.'

'He just slips back into his trousers, fixes his hair in the mirror and off he goes. Just like that. No bathroom time. No tissue. No shower. Nothing! So then again, I think, well maybe he's got some special mechanism for cleaning it in his car? You know how people keep breath mints or dental floss in their purse? But more like one of those brushes you use to clean out glass jars and he forgot to bring it?

'Maybe it's just a bit too graphic to bring out on a first date?'

'What is?'

'This foreskin nozzle brush.'

'Well I think it was a little too late to try to be demure now. If he had it with him, I'd rather he use it than walking out and having me think he doesn't clean himself. He was just inside me for a good hour.'

'Maybe you might need the foreskin nozzle brush now?'

'No but thank you for reminding me. I'll probably need to book an appointment somewhere. Again, this internet stuff, you never know where these people come from. We were safe, don't worry. I saw him put the thing on and made sure he was still wearing it after he was done. So, don't get onto one of your HIV rants please. I can't bear it today. Like that cock needed any more layers to it, but still I insisted he wear it. He seemed fine about it though. I always find it so uncomfortable when they hesitate. Or the excuses about having some non-existent latex allergy or something.'

'You know my sentiments on this.'

'Yes, of course. Never date a man who is rude to the waiter and never trust a guy who wants to bareback on a Wednesday.'

'Something like that, yes.'

'Well you've nothing to worry yourself over. We didn't come within five feet of a restaurant and I am pretty sure that sad little, deflated, cum-filled balloon is still wallowing at the bottom of my bathroom bin wondering what happened. Such short little lives condoms have, don't they? Like Mayflies. One short, sharp burst of euphoric pleasure, preceded by an hour of pumping and humping and then a life of saggy, soggy nothingness. But don't worry, I gave that poor thing the time of its life.'

'I'm sure it's incredibly appreciative.'

'I'm sure it is too. I would be if I were a Mayfly. Destined to only 24hrs on earth. To have been lucky enough to be plucked from obscurity, by me. Me and Darren from Bankstown. Daz_1983.'

'Darren?'

'I mean, yes. I assume that's what Daz is short for?'

'I'd have said Darryl.'

'Don't be ridiculous. Who names a child Darryl these days?'

'I know a few Darryls.'

'Fathers? Uncles? Landscape gardeners with red faces, swollen noses and skin cancers on their ears?'

'Mostly, I guess.'

'Well no not Daz_1983. It couldn't be Darryl.'

'Despite the name and despite the foreskin, how was it?'

'Overall?'

'Yes.'

'Interesting.'

'How?'

'Well I guess I, along with every homosexual boy in Australia, am well versed in the conditions of fucking a closeted man. The patchy, inconsistent personal details, lack of eye contact, the heavy air of immediate regret once it's all over.'

'It comes with the territory.'

'But this one seemed to take it to another level. First of course came the insistence of both party's blind and devoted faith to the church of Straight Acting. Was I straight acting? Was I non-scene? Was I femme?'

'And your answer?'

'Well at that point in time, I was feeling rather manly. So, I answered accordingly.'

'Good girl.'

'I said, yes. Yes, I was straight acting. Yes, I was non-scene.'

'The delicious irony of this situation always is that the man who insists on having sex exclusively with only the most masculine of men, is actually probably the gayest of them all.'

'How do you mean?'

'Well if you happen to find something with a more effeminate aesthetic or behaviour sexually attractive, it would mean you are attracted to the feminine as a whole, meaning there might be traces of you that would sit further towards the bisexual or pansexual on the great Spectrum of Fucking. And given that the fundamental basis of being homosexual is attraction to the same sex, saying you're only into only the most masculine of men, the kind of men that sit to the extremes of only one end of that spectrum, makes you in essence, an extremely homosexual man. So, it's contradictory of them to think, and we know they do, that as man only fucking men who look and behave like men, makes you less gay.'

'Well last night, I was the most passionate and devoted follower of the teachings of masculinity. To the Church of Straight Acting. This, despite my predilection towards rough anal sex, towards early MGM musicals, towards Judy, Marilyn, Elizabeth, Audrey…'

'But I guess he didn't need to know all that, did he?'

'Absolutely not. And that's the beauty of all this. It's not lying. We aren't lying. We are just being selective with the truth. As they are.'

'Very good darling.'

'So, we proceeded. And after receiving a small stream of images of yours truly in only the best lighting this apartment can provide, he instantly insisted we speak on the phone.'

'And I imagine these pictures were candid shots of yourself just lounging about in the garden, with flowers in your hair, reading 19th Century Romantic poetry?'

'Yes. And my hole.'

'Ah yes, the hole.'

'That one of me bent over in the mirror and another rather extreme close up of it.'

'I figured. Some of your more restrained shots still though by the sounds of it.'

'I thought so. I didn't want to give too much away. One must maintain a touch of mystery still amongst all this technology.'

'What was he wanting to speak about?'

'Nothing in particular it seemed.'

'So just a check in really, that the tone of your voice was aligned enough to The Church of Straight Acting before he committed any further?'

'I imagine so.'

'Well, appears you passed with flying colours then?'

'If anyone can switch it on and switch it off darling, it's me. I can go from Bob Mackie to Bob Dylan in the bat of an eye lash.'

'So, he liked your pictures, he clarified you didn't sound like Betty Boop and then he shows up at your front door?'

'Well, not quite yet. He then insists I meet him in that car park opposite my place.'

'Honesty, I'm exhausted already.'

'I know, but I was kind of getting off on the thrill of it all. Anyway, he shows up in this ridiculous car looking like something out of a poorly financed Science Fiction film. This fluorescent cobalt blue colour with this huge winged thing flying off the back of it.'

'Oh god.'

'The wheels were polished aluminium chrome that even in the pitch black of that car park, I could see glistening from the distance. And to top it all off, the damn thing had green fucking neon lights glowing from the bottom. Like it was about to lift off into space. Can you imagine? The whole scene was so fucking camp. And yet, inside, was this poor guy, too closeted to even show his face sat in this George Jetson looking thing in a park in Central Sydney. Honestly. So, I wander over, still in character, not breaking my Method as bestowed by The Church and slump myself down in the passenger seat and utter the most heterosexual thing I could muster up.'

'Hey bro?'

'Hey bro indeed! And that was it. He was like a putty in my hand after that. So, I jerked him off in the car for a minute and then suggested we continue on inside, which by that stage he was so fucking turned on, he couldn't say no. But the whole closet pantomime just carried on. The lights had to be off, the blinds had to be closed, I had to be on my stomach, with my head buried in the pillows, I couldn't talk, I couldn't turn around. I was essentially just a floating asshole, in the darkness of that room. An anonymous vessel to be filled by anyone willing.'

'Or anything for that fact.'

'True.'

'I don't quite understand what the point is then of going through the rigmarole of being on an exclusively gay dating site and finding a fuck only to bury them in pillows and try convince yourself that it's your girlfriends ass looking up at you in the dark?'

'My thoughts exactly, but Christ, you should have seen this specimen's physique. Like some mythical god etched out of a marble slab, I tell you.

'Which god?'

'Who is that Rugby player that is being slammed in the media now for shoving his tongue down a girls throat in a stairwell?'

'Rugby? Darling, think about what you just asked me.'

'No c'mon, you can't have not heard about it. Christ what's his name? Stewart, something. I think he plays for the Sea Eagles.'

'I'm sorry are you still in character? What is this?'

'Darling, honestly. Open your browser, Google him now. You will see what I mean. But Google him shirtless. Brett Stewart, I think his name is?'

'One moment please...

Ah, yes. Now I know.'

'That is what was inside me last night. Give or take. This gorgeous, thick body, with shoulders that barely taper in at the waist. The kind that just struts out and down like a brick. And smooth. Not a single hair to be found on that torso.'

'So, when do you envisage you'll see Daz_1983 again?'

'Oh, imminently I'm certain. I gave him the ride of his life. He did leave in a bit of a hurry though, but I assumed it was only due to the fact it was a school night and he did have to go back to that town of his. Where even is Bankstown anyway? I hear of it from time to time, but I never see it on any maps or anything useful or remotely glamorous.'

'Who knows. It can't be that far from Surry Hills though if he's willing to drive to you on a Wednesday night.'

'Well look at what was at the end of the journey. But I mean, you never overhear anyone in a cafe saying, Oh, I've just been to the most stunning restaurant in Bankstown. Or Oh Cate Blanchet and Andrew Upton have just bought a place in Bankstown. It must just be a holding pen full of resting hetero-humans. People in houses going to Bankstown to sleep before they all wake up and migrate to the city for the day. I imagine it's quite hard to get a soy latte.'

'Didn't you grow up in Gosford?'

'What's your point?'

'No nothing. So, what else do we know about Darryl?'

'He was, so he said, a junior architect. Whatever that's supposed to mean. Like he's only allowed to design small houses for the time being or something. A Junior Architect is not an unimpressive thing but what interesting things could a Junior Architect possibly be working on, out in Bankstown? I just pictured him sat in some sweaty office on a waxy, brown desk shoved in the corner under blinding fluorescent lights boxed in by these towers of soiled, misshapen piles of years' worth of papers, while he madly scribbles away at the design of an adult learning centre.'

'Poor Darryl.'

'So, given he's now had a taste for civilisation, I assume he'll be knocking again soon. Or clicking. I'm not quite sure how this all works now. Regardless, I am sure it'll be soon.'

'Yes, so how does this work now? How does he contact you again?'

'On the internet I assume. I have no idea. We didn't exchange numbers. I don't think he's quite there yet.'

'Well I wish you all the best. You, Darryl and his unretractable foreskin.'

'Well that's rather kind of you. Unusually kind, I must say for you, this time of the morning, but appreciated, nonetheless. And what of you and your evening?'

'Well, whilst you were finding your way amongst the undulations of a stranger's orifice, I was relaxing at home.'

'Alone?'

'Yes alone.'

'Well, we can't all be so desirable down the line of an ethernet cable can we, dear? Yes, sometimes the pheromones still show up in the binary code of robots, don't they?'

'Like a virus?'

'Like perfume. Permeating through each individual character, whirling around the curves and lines like smoke through a forest.'

'Yes, I'd imagine you were quite well versed in a language that had nothing to offer in the way of a script other than long rods and gaping holes.'

'Fluent as the day is long.'

'Actually, speaking of invasive perfumes, is your mother still coming to town this weekend? Our Stella?'

'Christ, I forgot about that. When did I say she was coming?'

'Saturday.'

'Yes, that sounds about right. Seems to be one of the only days of the week is acceptable to start drinking before 11am under the auspices of fucking brunch.'

'What will you do?'

'Most likely that.'

'And what is the reason this time you think?'

'Nothing, I hope. Just her usual monthly check- in. She will come, I will meet her at The Woollahra Hotel. She will ask me how I am, drink excessively, wince at even the slightest mention of my lifestyle as she calls it, and then make some hasty, inarticulate comment to instantly change the topic.'

'I've never understood this though. Between that fucking beehive hairdo, her Chanel pant suits and pearl necklace, your mother essentially gets about in drag. How is she still not comprehending your lifestyle?'

'This little phase of mine?'

'Yes.'

'I think she could care less about where I stick my cock, but it's the peripheral things that come with that. Because she is just a textbook corporate overachiever and because she isn't seeing gays running multinational investment banks or speaking at the UN, to her this is an indication I am residing myself to a somewhat mediocre existence.'

'Well that's rather 80's of her. How does she know that gays aren't doing these things?'

'It is, and she doesn't, but I try not to hassle her too much. She is just a product of her circumstance. She loves me unconditionally, I know. But all those years spent in high rise offices of horrible private equity firms in Sydney, Hong Kong, New York, surrounded only by men. The worst kind of men. Men whose only purpose in life at the time was to make more money than the guy sitting in the cubicle next to them. Vast sums of money at whatever cost. She worked for them. Never with them. I don't think you come out of that unscathed. She has some scars.'

'Well she has a razor-sharp sense of style; I'll give her that.'

'Yes, that's our Stella. Chic. Tight. Dark. Severe. Expensive.'

'I wonder if she might take things more seriously if you were to introduce her to someone you were seeing?'

'I doubt it. But maybe. He'd have to have more money than God to impress her.'

'How could she have such high hopes for a man for you when she has almost made a career out of chewing through them?'

'I don't know.'

'And what do you think she would make of our Darryl?'

'Well, y'know in a funny way, every man I seem to meet, one of the many litmus tests I put him through in my head, is how he would survive a brunch with Stella.'

'And what of this one?'

'Instant failure. But, something about that kind of excites me. Whilst assessing the brand of his shoes, watch and belt with a hawk like precision, she'd sit there and ask WASPY questions like where his family were 'originally' from and where he studied, the whole time building a judgemental picture of him in her head, but nodding along smiling to his answers anyway. And then finally, that unavoidable probe she knows she has to ask to keep the conversation running on that icing sugar level of superficiality but would rather dive under a bus than actually know the answer to.'

'So how do you two know each other?'

'Precisely.'

'And what will be your answer?'

'Well, what is always the answer when we are placed on the dock like this by naive heterosexuals? How do we sterilise the grime and muck that they have forced us to dwell within to secure a partner and regurgitate it back to them, so it is digestible to their white bread with margarine pallet? We met through friends, of course.'

'She is smart enough to know that is not true though.'

'But she is also smart enough not to ask anything further that she doesn't want to know the answer to. That her 20-year-old son is forced to spend his evenings on an internet chat room firing off shots of his cock and asshole to anonymous men across the city, in order to get some sort of physical contact.'

'Well darling, no one is chaining you to the desk, are they?'

'And what are the alternatives?'

'Well, I know of quite a few rather pleasant public urinals that you might be able to frequent to secure the same result.'

'Exactly.'

'Well I do hope that one day she is able to meet Darryl. An architect is not an insignificant thing to be. Even a junior one. I doubt she would be that unimpressed. If that is, what he is claiming to be. Not sure how many architects have green neon lights under their car and chrome wheels.'

'Well as I said. He is junior. Let's hope he is just still in the process of shaking off all these little adolescent accessories and he is on his way to becoming the corporate climber we, and Stella, hope he always

wanted to be. Anyway, darling I best go, Dr Huxley
is wrapping up and I'm dying for a cigarette. Will
chat with you when I'm home.'

* * * * *

'Shouldn't you be getting ready? You're supposed to
be meeting me in an hour.'

'I'm still at the gallery.'

'What? It's 7:30?'

'I know but there are some people here lurking
around. I think they might actually buy something
God forbid. Anyway, it won't take me long to get
ready.'

'Well that's a lie. But you're in luck. I only just got
home myself after I got stuck talking to Dr Huxley
after class. Asking for cigarettes as usual in the
courtyard. Christ he is weird. Banging on about all
kinds of shit. LSD of all things. I think he's not quite
all there, to be honest. Poor thing.'

'I think you need to be, to do what he does.'

'Yes, teaching art history does require a small dusting of insanity to do well.'

'While I'm waiting for these people to leave, I have to tell you something. I went for a swim at the pool earlier today on my lunch break and I finally managed to end up speaking to him.'

'Who darling?'

'This guy I have been telling you about for the past two months. This beautiful, dark, middle aged man that I keep locking eyes with across the floor of the change room, who follows me around that swimming pool like a lost puppy but then instantly scurries away the second I even gesture that we speak. Him.'

'Oh yes! Fabulous.'

'We spoke.'

'Tell me then. What was said finally?'

'Not much, but it was a fairly decent effort on his behalf considering all we've done up until now is stare at each other's cocks from across the pool.'

'I see. So, he's actually acknowledged you now?'

'She's acknowledged me plenty. But for some reason it's never gone past the silent fucking of one another with our eyes.'

'Well the fact I imagine there are a selection of poor, unassuming heterosexual men in there actually trying to shower and change, doesn't help with the mood.'

'But there's been times where we are alone and still nothing. I feel like in those moments he becomes even more hesitant to speak strangely. It's equal parts incredibly odd and adorable.'

'This is all very sweet but honestly, you need to get into this online stuff. You've been drooling over this guy for ages now and for what? You know I saw Darren's cock in the first three minutes of chatting to him on that site? Now that is the speed with which modern women like us need to operate. We can't be led on by all this subtly in winks and elongated glares across a shower block. It's incredibly tiresome.'

'I'll let you know when I am ready to take the plunge darling.'

'As you wish.'

'I noticed him swimming in the lane next to me the second I got into the water that day and I couldn't let my eyes leave him the entire time. He has this beautiful dark skin and his hair is this jet-black colour almost to the point of being blue. All buzzed at the sides and a bit longer on the top that the water that seems to run off the second he surfaces again for air. Like duck down. He was slow. Wide, big stretches of these thick arms rising and falling out of the water, gentle kicks and deep long breaths. He would be constantly eclipsed by all the other idiots there, blasting through their work out, clock watching at every lap, racing to get back to their office cubicle in time. He was swimming without goggles I remember too that day, like he was better off without them. As if he felt more normal under the water than above it. Just gliding so freely through it.'

'How old is he?'

'He must be upwards of 40, but just in very good shape. You can tell he is a bit older, the way his body sits. The way men's chests look sometimes when they've finally been pumped to their maximum size and start to fold over themselves at the ribs. Not sagging but just collapsing under their own weight. He isn't tall but just stacked like an athlete that seems to have calmed down his training. He's always dressed very casually. T-shirts and chinos. Usually just sandals as well. No matter what time of day it is. Never in a suit. I never see him leaving in a hurry or dashing off into the city. It's like he has all the time in the world to be there. Just to swim. He must have caught me staring that first day.'

'Because you were staring?'

'Because when he finally was done and he was pulling himself out of the water, he turned back to look at me and smiled before disappearing into the change rooms. And that was it. Every time I saw him after that a smile would turn into a nod, then a soft mumbling Hello, then finally today some actual words. Fractured sentences. Me talking awkwardly over him before he'd finished them, trying to not let a lull happen that might indicate it was time to go or cut it all short. I could feel my knees shaking beneath my towel. I hope he couldn't see.'

'And does this retired, middle aged athlete have a name perchance?'

'I don't know his name yet.'

'Ha!'

'Oh, fuck off you would? You're still trying to figure out what fucking Daz_1983 might mean for Christ's sake. And for the record I hope it is Darryl not Darren. I hope he does, eventually turn into a fat, wobbling old man with a swollen alcoholic nose smattered with rosacea.'

'Calm down. I'm only teasing. What shall we call her then? This elusive pool man of yours?'

'I'll have a think.'

'Fine. So, what did he actually say in the end?'

'It was quick and vague. How was my swim? See you tomorrow etc. Nothing of consequence.'

'Well I'm glad you've both graduated from simply staring at each other from across the change room with your dicks poking out from beneath your speedos.'

'I am too, but he was so impossibly nervous still, even fully clothed and in broad daylight. Maybe he's married or something? He seemed nervous. So nervous. To the point of distraction, like his mother was about to catch him mid-wank or something.'

'It's nice to know you have that effect on people with and without clothes on, isn't it?'

'Yes.'

'Well he sounds like a rather interesting man. I can't wait to meet her.'

'I don't see that's going to be an option anytime soon. It's taken this fucking long to get a proper sentence out of her, I doubt she is ready for the onslaught of yourself. There's something a little delicate about it. I think I need to tread lightly before you go bulldozing in with your ManHunt lifestyle and partners with unretractable foreskins and glowing cars.'

'Suit yourself. So, what are our plans this evening? I feel like we deserve a bit of glamour.'

'Yes agreed.'

'Doll ourselves up and twirl.'

'Well I say we start at Flinders Bar for happy hour, twirl about with your art school comrades. Y'know, feel beautiful for a moment.'

'Perfect, yes then we can dash across the street to get our stamps at ARQ, back to Flinders to finish off the happy hour and then back to ARQ for Drag for Dollars. How does that sound?'

'Why don't we go to The Ruby Rabbit for a twirl in between? It's new and just around the corner.'

'Isn't The Ruby Rabbit a lesbian bar?'

'No. Impossible.'

FRIDAY

'I fucking told you it was a Lesbian bar.'

'The Ruby Rabbit?'

'Yes!'

'Darling don't be so dramatic. There were about three lesbians in there. And we don't even know if they were actual lesbians. You know women don't like to label themselves. They may have just been civilian females.'

'Still.'

'What was the problem with it anyway?'

'Nothing. It just doesn't quite seem like a lesbian bar.'

'What should a lesbian bar look like?'

'I don't know, like maybe some power tools tastefully strung about. Some Melissa Etheridge on the jukebox. More beer taps.'

'I ah, hmm.'

'Do or do not, I say. Don't try. If you're going to make a lesbian bar, make it a fucking lesbian bar. Make it really lesbian. It was a bit too subtle for me.

All that tasteful artwork, expensive furniture and nice-looking bartenders. Felt very demure. I noticed though that they glued the toilet seats down in the bathrooms. Seemed like a good attempt at trying to force the clientele to assimilate. Little did they know; I sit down to piss anyway.'

'I'm sorry you felt deceived like that.'

'Maybe there just aren't enough lesbians in this city to sustain a bar wholly dedicated to them?'

'I'm certain there is. I don't think you know enough lesbians.'

'I know of plenty.'

'Your life is very exclusively populated by only gay men.'

'And what lesbians do you know?'

'A few. Danielle is a lesbian.'

'Is she though?'

'Yes, she claims to be at least.'

'I wonder what bars she goes to?'

'Is it kind of strange that we don't know?'

'No. Lesbians are as much of an anomaly to us as we are to them.'

'I guess so.'

'The reality is, we have precious little in common with lesbians, aside from being societal refugees. We really should be sworn enemies, given how opposing our desires are. But alas, we live in harmony in the gutters and shadows, side by side.'

'I think it's sweet.'

'I hear they have a secret floor in that bar.'

'In The Ruby Rabbit?'

'Yes. Another bar that only the most beautiful and skinny people are allowed in. Like Megan Gale and Charlotte Dawson.'

'Can the lesbians go there too?'

'Absolutely not. Not even you or I could go in there. It's called De Nom. Apparently the interior looks like the hall of mirrors in Versailles and all the champagne is poured from magnums by bronzed men in white linen shirts and tight trousers and cocaine is served on silver coasters with metal straws. This sort of Caligula-esque den of hedonism and debauchery.'

'You're talking about a bar on Oxford Street, sandwiched between a sex shop called The Toolshed and a kebab stand?'

'Yes. The very same. But that is the most titillating bit about it. It appears so close within the reach of us mere mortals. It's not some impenetrable penthouse stacked on the roof of the Four Seasons or a yacht moored out in Neutral Bay or anything. It's right there. There's a secret door to it somewhere inside The Ruby Rabbit, a back entrance or some goods elevator that you get access to that takes you there. And all you can see from the street are some blacked out windows.'

'Well I don't know how they could be making enough money from only letting such a select group of people in. This isn't exactly fucking Rodeo Drive. Aside from the aforementioned skinny and beautiful people, who else is being let in?'

'Well the lesbians in the peasant's bar appear to be bank-rolling the cocaine coaster upstairs. If only they knew, right? This fantasy land of fame and success was just above them. It's all rather glamorous if you ask me. This city needs some glamour.'

'There's plenty of glamour to be found, but you're just not going to find it at the bottom of the steam room in Bodyline, are you?'

'I beg your pardon?'

'I'm just teasing darling. But I did just assume that's where you ended up, after I lost you last night in ARQ."

'You assumed correctly but you didn't lose me. It was 4am, I left.'

'Well the last I remember seeing you was as we were watching Shirley Valentine shake her tits to River Deep Mountain High, yet again, and then it gets rather hazy after that.'

'Shirley always comes on at 1am so there's a good few hours you seem to have lost then? Did you wake up in your own bed? I imagine so. It was Thursday, you usually seem to peak more on Sunday's with the retail assistant crowd.'

'I missed Shirley. But I've seen that dick fall out of her dress one too many times. I was at the bar most likely trying to avoid it.'

'Smart.'

'Who won Drag for Dollars?'

'Natasha Knowles with a flawless rendition of Love at First Sight by Kylie Minogue.'

'She's a star that girl. She'll go far.'

'Well I am not sure how far the $100 prize money will take her, but yes she is stunning.'

'Baby Drag Queens aside, darling you should have seen it though, just before they cleared the stage for the show, just before, I was there, front and centre. Empress of that catwalk…'

'Could we classify that as a catwalk? I think it might actually just be a fire exit or something?'

'Nothing short of spectacular. Honestly. Some awful song had just finished, something that sounded like a mixture between Gwen Stefani and a woodchipper with a police siren in the background, that naturally everyone was losing their mind to. Least of which the bottoms as per usual. But then it started...'

'Oh god...'

'Those first few bars. Unmistakable in their ability to be heard even over the mechanical churning of a fading Gwen and a woodchipper. Seven notes. That's all. Pumped from that little glass box shoved right into the corner of that short, sweaty room, containing the only real person in control of our feelings for the night. A relative switchboard for our emotions. And really it hadn't been proving particularly fruitful until that point. Then it all came together. I'd been high for a while already, but the residual Mandy began bubbling once again in the pit of my stomach. Fumes rising up my neck and then finally filling the head with that woolly sensation of pure and utter bliss. Yes, at that moment, those seven bars, it was me and only me on that stage darling, baring my soul to the world, on the precipice of delivering the greatest you-had-to-be-there moment of the last decade.'

'Young Hearts, Run Free, by Candy Stanton?'

'Young Hearts, Run Free by Candy Stanton. The one and only. The alpha and omega of all dance tracks. On in that pit of misery that is downstairs at ARQ. A place that, if we're fucking lucky, we may hear a snippet of Donna Summer at 4am or some mash up between Diana Ross and something else. But there she was, for a brief, fleeting moment. And there I was. Ready. Arms out at right angles to the floor. Legs locked, neck craned, and jaw lined popped...

'And then they played the remix?'

'And then they played the fucking remix!'

'I'm sorry darling. Honestly, where do they find these DJ's?''

'Honestly. Alas, it was not meant to be. The people weren't ready. The world wasn't ready…'

'Will it ever be?'

'A shame really. But anyway, I won't be accused of disappearing. I made a concerted effort to find you, say goodnight and then be on my way. If I recall you were being bent over a pool table somewhere towards the back of the club.'

'Ah yes, I remember now. Actually, if I recall correctly also, you were with someone who looked like they wanted to bend you over a pool table too? Quite tall. My memory is little hazy.''

'That would have been Darren.'

'Darryl from Bankstown?'

'Yes. The very one.'

'Actually inside ARQ? Goodness, well aren't we making headway with the closet?'

'Well not exactly, he lasted all of about 3 minutes and then insisted we leave. He was even wearing a hat. Can you believe, this awful baseball cap thing that was pulled right down over his face. I felt like just screaming at him, Darling you're inside, the damage is done! Just enjoy it. But he stood there like some beaten, caged animal, arms folded all curled up inside himself, his eyes darting back and forth across the room as if some other thing from Bankstown might have walked in and exposed him. I mean, it was all rather sexy, to a point, but very hard to manage.'

'I can imagine. So how did you go from fucking in the dark with your face buried in some pillows, to being at ARQ together?'

'We chatted briefly online yesterday afternoon and I mentioned we were going to be there, and mostly jokingly said he should come. He hadn't really even responded properly. It was quite a shock to see him actually just appearing out of the shadows like that.'

'A shock that he was able to recognise you mostly I imagine without the pillows. Did you introduce him to anyone?'

'No, he caught me whilst I was darting off to the bathroom, so I was alone. I think he might have been waiting for it.'

'So where did he insist you go after 3 minutes?'

'Bodyline.'

'Right...'

'I know.'

'I don't understand how in an exercise of trying to remain discreet, going from the largest gay night club in the city to the largest gay sauna in the city, is any better?'

'Well, I guess he just laid eyes on me and then couldn't contain himself and just simply had to address the issue right there and then. And it is just next door after all.'

'After paying the twelve-dollar entry fee?'

'Well, he did. I get a student discount.'

'So, this is our version of an affair in a seedy motel I guess is it?'

'Yes, and much more affordable.'

'Was he aware of what it was before going in? Did he suggest it?'

'He seemed to suggest it weirdly but without saying it, if that makes sense. Insinuating that we should go somewhere else, to continue. But not home.'

'Well aside from that, what were the fucking options? Actually, don't answer that.'

'I can be very resourceful at a bus stop.'

'Or a dumpster.'

'The gay sauna is a brilliant concept. It really is one of the last vestiges of gay male life that can't be diluted or mainstreamed isn't it? I mean, where are the lesbian saunas? Hell, where are the straight saunas? It's again one of those dark, timeless spaces where one is quite literally stripped of everything that we have covered ourselves with as adults; clothes, jewellery, classist pronunciations and we are forced to walk through those corridors, naked, silent and exposed. For a closet I imagine it's very much a form of self-flagellation. There are no houses, no families, no cars, no lawns, no suits or no friendship circles to bolster their synthetic image of themselves. It's just them and their cocks under an overly bleached bath towel.'

'I suppose so. And so how did your closet handle it?'

'Like a pro.'

'How closet can he actually be then if he is just sort of swanning into fucking Bodyline like it's a coffee shop?'

'I think he had a very naive sense of trust in the people that go there that there's some sort of unsaid rule that no one talks about Bodyline outside of Bodyline.'

'Well, that's wildly untrue. I mean, us here now, case in point.'

'Exactly. But let him think that. Let him think we are all keeping his secrets locked away with us. His best interests at heart, always.'

'So how was it in the end?'

'Lovely. Rough and tumble as usual. We started in one of those rooms with the leather beds and soap dispensers full of lube and then wandered down to the jacuzzi and then tried a second time in one of the cages next to the porn room.'

'The cage with the sling?'

'No, it was occupied.'

'It always seems to be doesn't it?'

'These days yes. Maybe slings are back. I find the whole thing very retro personally.'

'So again, I question his need for total discretion with you if he is wanting to fuck you in a cage?'

'It wasn't particularly busy.'

'It's beside the point really.'

'When was the last time you were at Bodyline?"

'It must be months now. Probably just when they started putting Poppers into the air-conditioning system. It all became a bit much.'

'Too effective for you?'

'Something like that yes. That overpowering mixture of the smell of chlorine permeating up through the floors from the spa in the basement, amyl nitrate whirling around in the air vents, cheap cologne from the punters and that subtle but always and forever discernible smell of shit, just became a little overwhelming…'

'Well I find it all terribly sexy still. My dick tingles just walking past the front entrance sometimes. So, I believe I left there at around 6am and was home in bed by 7am. So, nothing too outrageous really.'

'And what of Darryl?'

'Darren, I left in the changing room. He was taking far too long, pissing about with his clothes and phone, I couldn't stand it, so I just said goodbye and went on my way home and fell in a heap.'

'Do you think he might have gone back in for more?'

'Hmm. Hard to say. Possibly.'

'Does that bother you?'

'Should it?'

'Well, assuming he did, he's clearly used you as a bit of a crutch to get in there in the first place then.'

'I hadn't really thought about that to be honest.'

'Really?'

'What recourse have I got for demanding he follow me out anyway? We met 36hrs prior.'

'I'm just saying, again, don't become this man's little window into the gay scene. He must go through it like we all did. He can't string you along as his plaything to skip the line and then toss you aside once he's in. It's not fair.'

'Thank you, darling. That's very considerate of you.'

'Just please be careful.'

'I will.'

* * * * *

'How is work?'

'Awful. Made all the more awful by last night's efforts.'

'Where are you today?'

'Veronica has me sat downstairs in the street level gallery, sweating in fucking trousers and a business shirt. You know how she hates shorts. I don't know what her theory is in even having this place open. She is so deluded to think people are wandering the streets of Woollahra on a Friday, at midday looking to drop money on art like it was a pair of jeans. It's just all a bit dated isn't it?

'I don't know if people ever did that though?'

'Me either. But you know some people always just have this grand sense of nostalgia. Like the world was always easier and more comfortable, or that people were better off or and had more money in a time you weren't part of. That's her. Though I am certain flogging expensive pictures was just as hard in the 70's as it was now.'

'What's she selling this week?'

'I am sat surrounded by a couple of oversized canvas' of oil paintings of whales by Johnathon Delafield-Cook and a randomly positioned lithograph by Lucian Freud. Total value of the room is $800,000.'

'And what's your daily target?'

'I think since I started here last December, I've seen one picture leave the gallery. And I am almost certain it came straight back.'

'Where does her cash come from, you think? I have always assumed it actually costs her money to run that gallery rather than it be any sort of commercially viable kind of business.'

'Who knows. She talks like some exiled Duchess of Marlborough, so Christ knows what kind of money she has access to here or back wherever in the UK she is from.'

'She can't have ever been married, because I only ever see her surrounded by the oldest and queerest of men who speak only to my crotch when she introduces me to them at those strange opening nights of hers.'

'Well, I think she's probably looking for payment after drinking all her booze for the past however many months.'

'That booze is free, and she should know better than to serve it at those ridiculous events of hers. What's she think that by plying people with a few diluted gin and tonics they're going to more easily part with their inherited cash? No. I'm the most interesting thing at those corpse ridden events. A drink is the least she can offer me for the substance I bring to it.'

'Well, I'm sure she's thankful you fill the room with such warmth and kindness. Despite not ever even feigning interest in what's on offer.'

'Why would I? She's a relic of a human, idolising a bygone era that has no place in 2007 or thereafter for that fact. She promotes art and artists based on their commercial viability and their appeal to customers, not on its substance or what they are trying to say. I don't actually know how you stand it to be honest.'

'Try getting a job once you've graduated from sitting and listening to Dr Huxley bang on about German Incest and Surrealism. See where the options are in this fucking city. This country.'

'You were supposed to be an artist, not an art dealer.'

'Yeah and eat how? Live where? Options were work at Cotton On and try to paint in the evening or get a job in the art world and then somehow make some headway into it from the inside.'

'And how is that going?'

'How is your art going? How is being a bartender coinciding with your strive for artistic genius?'

'I'm still in my information gathering phase. I am still being schooled in the art of art. I'm only in my first year at uni darling, you know that.'

'Well you'll find out soon enough how useless it is to be spoken at about it and all the time it takes from you. Time that you should be spending within it, creating, actually being an artist, and not being lectured on how to be an artist. The industry of art professors and art teachers is fed by people who studied art, didn't become artists and so then became teachers, to teach people who, will probably not become artists themselves and then go onto become teachers of it yet again.'

'The first thing people will ask you once you start trying to put yourself out there as an artist is, Where did you study? Where did you turn from a child into an artist? How did you metamorphosize from finger painting, into art? It can't say nothing. Your ideas aren't allowed to come from nowhere. The answer cannot be nowhere. Regardless of what you take from whatever institution that hands you that degree at the end, your resume needs to begin somewhere. It's just indulging the world.'

'But why? And what for? This country doesn't even have anything to offer anyone who is remotely creatively inclined. It has beauty but everywhere, that beauty is always only ever as deep as the layers of sand on the beach. It stops at the waterline of its coasts and the topsoil of its forests. All you need to do is scrape it back with the tip of your finger and you'll see that beneath there is nothing. There is no undercurrent of struggle here. The first sign of good weather and all people care about is getting to the shores of the closest beach. It's forever on island time. This country, this advanced Western democracy, this entire continent has the social mentality of a remote tropical island resort built for fat American tourists on cruise ships.'

'But plenty of warm climates have been the epicentre of artistic movements.'

'Yes, but the beach is the ultimate symbol of affluence here. It's the Australian equivalent of a sedentary aristocratic life spent on neoclassical chaise lounges in lush gardens, under vast willow trees being fed grapes by concubines and stroked down by olive skinned youths. To be so successful, so wealthy, so above and beyond the need to function within the daily routine of society, to wash, to work, to worry, to have some purpose that gets us up and out of our beds every day, is all obliterated when we are, at the beach. Do we not sit and stare at the vast expanse of nothingness that is the horizon of the ocean and say to ourselves, It doesn't get any better than this? So why strive for anything more? Why even allow our minds to think there is another level of existence to live on, when we have reached the nirvana of life? The beach is the final stop. And there is more than enough of it for every single person in this country to feel like they have reached that stop. It is not for a select few. So, you have a whole country who is sedated into an opioid like stupor by this strange perception of success. Lulled into a sense of not having to try any harder than they already have because, why? What else is there that could compete with what is in front of them? This country will never have vast, aesthetic upheavals, it will never be the centre of a movement where its people have tapped into the spirit of a time, producing art and fashion and literature that speaks of it. It's not built for it. And there is no desire. There is no need. And an absence of necessity means an absence of innovation.'

'God that's depressing.'

'That Godforsaken bar you work at is a perfect example of all of this. That beautiful, multi-million-dollar bar built into the side of a cliff looking over Bondi beach full of vile old men.'

'It's not that bad.'

'It's awful darling, you hate it. Admit it.'

'It pays well, and the views are lovely. There are far worse places to work than The Bondi Hotel darling.'

'It's a supposed members club, that wouldn't even allow women to enter until last year. A place, where, only last week you told me a formal complaint was lodged against a man for wearing jeans that were too tight.'

'It's mindless, evening work, that gives me my days to spend how I wish. I pull beers for fat, sun damaged men whose only worry is whether or not their froth to liquid ratio is right in their glass.'

'And then there's you; gorgeous, creative, fluid, bright young thing with all these aspirations to be something, waiting on them hand and foot. Being yelled at about fucking beer froth and mocked when you glide past them on your toes. The Bondi Hotel again encapsulates so much about this country. Multi-million-dollar views, but the second you turn back to face the place from within, it's just full of a gaping sad nothingness.'

* * * * *

'What time has Veronica got you in the gallery tonight?'

'7pm'

'Really?'

'Stephen Radley has just walked in.'

'Christ. What's he doing there?'

'Looking for some art I presume?'

'Well I hope you're wearing your tightest trousers. He's got more money than God.'

'He's not gay.'

'Pfft, that's not what I heard. But regardless darling, from a distance, that gorgeous frame of yours is just so feminine. You never know what he might think.'

'Rich people are strange, aren't they?'

'Yes, they're better than us. That's what it is.'

'No, it's like they don't know how to function properly. He comes in here twice a month, a small gallery in the eastern suburbs of Sydney and looks about as if to say, I need to open my own door, do I? Why hasn't someone offered me tea yet? And Veronica plays up to it all plenty. I can see him walking around now looking lost and glazed.'

'How long have you worked for her now?'

'It'll be 10 months next week.'

'Does that include the 2 weeks she took you to London?'

'Shall we not?'

'Oh please! It's actually one of my favourite stories.'

'No.'

'Darling, it's not your fault you're so irresistible to both sexes and that she wasn't to know you were a nasty queer. I mean, what straight men are there left in the art world? If ever there was one. She should have known better. But I do love the tenacity of an older woman pursuing a younger man. There is something just so scandalous about it. Reverse the roles and it's just such a dull story isn't it? Another old man, past his prime, bored with his wife and disappointed by his children, developing a wandering eye for the pretty nanny. It's bland. But a woman? Veronica. Successful, glamorous, established, single. Whisks you off to Europe, under the pretence of a very poorly disguised work trip. I mean what did you even do that whole time? It seems like you were dragged from brunch to lunch to dinner and cocktails.'

'I believe they call it networking.'

'Bah! Darling, how was a 20 something year old supposed to keep up with that kind of conversation? Hmm? Who was she meeting? MP's? London Property Tycoons? People with Viscount, Dame and Earl written before their names? She is not the kind of person to fuck around with her acquaintances. I'm sure there wasn't a single person at any of those tables, in any of those restaurants, during any point of that trip that couldn't, or wouldn't be able to instantly benefit her financially in her business. You are smart darling, you are charming and handsome beyond belief, but unfortunately in that instance, you were just a gorgeous little accessory contributing to the opulence of her larger pantomime.'

'Well I know that now.'

'Did you fuck her? I forget how this story ends.'

'No! Of course not.'

'You didn't feel obliged after a fully funded, business class-seated trip from Sydney to London, to give her at least a little poke?'

'Was I ever going to?'

'Poor thing. I can just picture her swanning around that expensive flat she rented for you both in South Kensington, leaving the door just slightly ajar as she showered. Wearing make-up to breakfast. Having just one too many Gin and Tonics at lunch in order to blame any slip of the tongue, intentional or not, on the booze.'

'Poor thing? You really don't need to feel sorry for her.'

'Yes, but it's just so tragic isn't it? I mean and then towards the end when she realises, she is going to return to Sydney sans poke, she dashes out to Harrods and drops a small fortune on that beautiful coat for you. And still nothing….'

'I was there to work.'

'Darling, please. And what was that Burberry trench for then? Your bonus?'

'I don't know. I didn't ask for it. It was the most ridiculous thing to buy. When would I ever fucking need it living in Sydney? God, I can still remember that pathetic look on her face when she brought it to me. I was locking my bedroom door towards the end; which I think she must have realised. I was just in the middle of changing on one of the last days and she kind of appears at the end of my bed with one of those oversized, thick cardboard luxury shopping bags and this stupid grin on her face. She slinks in and sits so far on the corner of the bed I swear she was basically squatting mid-air and just begins this awkward little monologue about me being a perfect travel partner and how much she's enjoyed my company. I mean, for a moment, it seemed sweet.'

'But then?'

'Well after she finished, and after I said a very heartfelt thank you, she just lingered on the bed corner. Her eyes were widening, and her lips began to pucker, and I swear in that moment she went from being a 48-year-old woman to a 16-year-old schoolgirl in a matter of seconds. Tightening her crossed legs and pulling her shoulders together, pressing out her tits. It was all incredibly bizarre to watch.'

'And then what?'

'I just stood up, still barely dressed and said Thank you, again and turned around and continued to get ready. What else could I do? What was she honestly expecting me to do? Fuck her for a jacket?'

'Well darling, it's about two thousand dollars' worth of jacket. It's not exactly a hoodie from Just Jeans.'

'So that is it, is it? 2000 is my going rate?'

'I wouldn't say that was an insignificant amount of money to be paid for a fuck. I am unfamiliar with going rates for these things though.'

'Well I guess we'll never know.'

'God I just love this story so much.'

'I'm glad.'

'The fact you still work for her after all that, is just the cherry on the cake too. When do you think the penny dropped?'

'I don't know. She knows now though. Maybe someone she knew, saw me out one tonight being a fool in Bodyline and told her. I couldn't say. But the minute we landed back in Sydney it all stopped. She became normal around me. Whatever that is.'

'Good to hear. And what of Mr. Radley now? Is he still there?'

'Yes, they're upstairs still. Talking about God knows what.'

'The state of that family fortune, built on what was it again? Biscuits or something?'

'Biscuits, yes. Precisely. $300 million net worth, all inherited from a biscuit factory. Radley's Crackers n Cheese. Radley's Mint Cream. Radley's Jam and Coconut Slice.'

'And so, what is he claiming to be now?'

'I believe he introduces himself currently as a Collector.'

'Not a politician?'

'Not anymore. God, remember that train wreck? One of the richest men in the country campaigning for a seat in one of the most affluent constituencies in the country, should have been like shooting fish in a barrel. But he still failed.'

'Poor thing. The heirs of great fortunes always seemed doomed to fail before they even begin, don't they? Rarely are they content with simply being rich. Raised in inconceivable wealth and privilege but then expected by their families to have some kind of drive to be independently successful.'

'It seems why he has found strange comfort in Veronica's little art related sphere of influence. He's just allowed to be rich. She pretends like he's got some genius eye for buying art, but really, she lets him walk out with whatever the fuck he wants.'

'What a joke.'

'He gave me the strangest look when he arrived today. I must have met him a dozen times before and he hasn't ever looked at me any way before but entirely through me like a Bell Boy or a person trying to collect money for the Red Cross.'

'Like what?'

'I don't know. I can't quite put my finger on it.'

'Like a fat old Lion that's just seen an injured gazelle?'

'Yes, something like that.'

'I fucking told you. He's eyeing you off darling. For Christ Sake, if Veronica gets a whiff of the fact that her biggest client wants a taste of her pretty little shop boy, she will have you dangling like a carrot for that fat old closet in no time.'

'I don't know where you get this shit from. Where in the world have you heard that Stephen Radley likes boys?'

'It's known babe. I know people who have seen him lurking around toilets in train stations. But I don't have to see it to believe it. I can sense it. I've got a nose for these things.'

'I'd rather not think about it.'

* * * * *

'Shouldn't you be at work? What are you doing online again?''

'I am at work darling. They've got me on reception. Tonight, I am the face of The Bondi Hotel. You're welcome.'

'Lord help them.'

'And I've managed to hack the front desk computer to be able to access this just to speak to you.'

'Thank you, my love.'

'Yes. The people in charge here seem to think that by just deleting the icon for Internet Explorer that it eliminates the ability for people to access a browser or any kind of messenger. I mean, that's autocratic control right there.'

'Well good for you for sticking it to the man. How is the evening progressing there?'

'Fine, the rest of the bar seems rather quiet for a Saturday, but we have quite a rowdy wedding going on in the function room. Two bridesmaids were arguing at the entrance before, right in front me. These two absolutely stunning women, in these powder purple Alex Perry lace dresses that looked like they would cost a small fortune, and just saying the vilest things to each other. Drunk out of their minds.'

'Lovely. How much does a wedding cost there? It can't be cheap with those views.'

'It depends what you want, but something quick, and simple and early which are three words anyone who actually wants a traditional wedding never wants to hear, would be in excess of $25,000. And it just goes up from there. I think on average you are looking at about $35-50,000.'

'That's obscene.'

'Completely. And the irony is, the bookings are only for 6hrs. 6pm - Midnight. And the bride is always late. Out getting pictures on the beach or getting her make-up re-touched. She will arrive at around 8pm, swan around anxiously making sure that her leery Uncle isn't groping her bridesmaids, try and greet everyone individually, thank them for coming and for the gift they will no doubt tell her they have got her, have maybe one glass of champagne and then this ridiculous tradition of speeches starts. And I have seen wedding speeches last hours. Hours. The groom's colleagues telling awkward anecdotes about a time he almost fucked his secretary, almost fucked a barmaid on a Euro trip, almost fucked his own cousin on a night out. And the whole time the bride is sitting there smiling pretending not to be internally falling apart at the thought of just having married this person.'

'And then a 20 something-year old queer little bartender flicks the lights on at midnight on the dot and kicks everyone out.'

'And it's all over. This day that people supposedly fantasize about from childhood, is over. And then we hand them the bill.'

'You know I always think about this fight we have for gay marriage and whether or not it's actually fit for purpose for us?'

'For gays?'

'For anyone who isn't straight.'

'Well we deserve it, there is no question.'

'Yes, but do we need it?'

'There are all sorts of legal benefits to being someone's spouse that we can't have simply as a fucking boyfriend.'

'Yes, but shouldn't we be asking the system to change to reflect that? Shouldn't there be some way to get that recognition that doesn't involve us having to slot ourselves into a process that was built solely for straight people? Like remember at Michael and Adrian's wedding? Adrian stood at the altar while Michael was walked down the aisle by his father. What was that all about?'

'Yes, I remember thinking about how they came to that decision. Seems figuring out who must play the woman is something we are forever being asked to consider.'

'A tradition that was at a time, the Father physically handing over his daughter to her new guardian. Literally a transfer of ownership from him to another man, is something we are expected to uphold?'

'I think we are free to choose which traditions we take on and which ones we would rather leave behind.'

'It's just disturbing to think that in Michael and Adrian's case, they were made to feel like it's what was expected of them if they wanted to have a wedding. Like it would be seen as any less of a wedding if they didn't do it. That the celebration of the very beginnings of their marriage was already lesser if they were to choose not to do it. And that perception comes from being raised in a world exclusively built by and made for, heterosexuals.'

'I don't mind the idea of being married, but I loathe the idea of a wedding.'

'I couldn't care for either.'

'Wait, something is happening again…'

'What?'

'Shouting. Let me see.'

* * * * *

'One of the security guards just caught two of the groomsmen doing cocaine in the toilets.'

'Oh wow.'

'The Bride is out the front of the bar on the street now screaming at them. Still in her gown. It's wild.'

'Where is the groom?'

'Nowhere to be seen. Apparently, some of the staff had been cutting a few of the guests off from the bar for being too rowdy but when they checked the $10,000 tab, it hadn't even been touched. So, the manager got suspicious and then busted two of the guys in the bridal party sharing a cubicle.'

'Straight people are so funny about cocaine.

'Like flies to shit.

'All that glamour of that wedding, all that money for a bag of powder, only to go and sniff it off the lid of a toilet? $300 a gram and a bump lasts all of what? An hour? If you wanna get high, like get fucking high I say. Don't piss about. But as if anyone at that party would be up for doing Mandy in a toilet. Doing coke is such a statement in this city. It's like offering someone a glass of prosecco or a glass of champagne. The end result is the same and barely anyone can tell the difference.'

'Oh Christ, now the Groom is here…'

'Excellent.'

'He's high as a kite too. Can barely keep his bottom jaw moving in time with the rest of his face.'

'What a joke.'

'I know. Seems to be trying to convince the bouncers to let the others back in. Clearly against the wishes of his new wife.'

'So what? They can do more coke?'

'All that money and time. And he goes and gets so written off he can probably barely remember signing the fucking registry.'

'And we aren't allowed to do it because it will undermine the sanctity of the institution?'

'Something like that.'

* * * * *

'So, you finally got the old bastard to cough up some money?'

'Yes, so it would seem. $60,000 worth. Nothing to sniff at.'

'Sorry I got your text when all that shit was still going down with that bridal party. I think they are packing up now, I won't be here much longer.'

'It's fine.'

'So how did it happen? Did Veronica just let you loose on him in the gallery? Also, it's nearly 11pm, what the fuck have you been doing all this time?'

'It kind of all took a bit of a time, so I actually only just got back home. I had to go via the gallery to drop off the cheque.'

'Drop off the cheque? What do you mean?'

'Well I think I told you once before that every now and again, Veronica lets Stephen Radley and a few other clients do this ridiculous thing where they take a painting or an artwork from her and have them installed in their houses to see if they like the way they look before buying them.'

'No, you didn't. But that's crazy. Like fucking rental car?'

'Something like that. But this cunt has so much bloody money, that once we've gone through the rigmarole of having it sent there and installed, he usually just can't be bothered having anything collected again and ends up buying whatever it is from her. So, when he does this, it's basically a sale in the bag for her. But this time, he apparently wanted to return it. It was an expensive one too obviously.'

'Is that what they were upstairs talking about for so long?'

'I imagine so. I went up there a few times to try and see what was going on, pretending to do something, but they were whispering mostly. I could tell it was tense. I just thought it was him trying to bargain with her on the price or something. Eventually Veronica appears looking kind of stressed and dishevelled from rubbing her hair too much, shoots me this manic awful looking smile like she is about to cry and laugh at the same time and sort of starts pushing me out the front door. Eventually Stephen waddles after us, looking kind of dazed and oblivious to the stress he is causing. As I turn around and see him try and shove himself past her and out in the street, she shoots me this look. This kind of glare where her eyes widened, and I swear she tried to mouth something at the same time but honestly, she needn't have bothered. I got it instantly.'

'What?'

'Not to even bother walking back into that gallery if I had that painting with me.'

'Ha. Well, that's rich. Why didn't she just go then if he's that special to her.'

'I have no idea. I felt like she may have exhausted the extent of her charm with him all that time spent upstairs and maybe he had grown bored of her. It was so desperate and pathetic like she was attempting to intimidate me but also beg me at the same time into doing this for her.

'Right. Well darling, when was the last time you saw her actually sell something?'

'Exactly. If her main cash cow is turning off the taps...'

'Also, not your problem.'

'Well, it's my job.'

'Hmmm…'

'So I stand out the front and watch her plant two breathy kisses on Radley as he passes her and proceeds to shove him politely out the door towards me as well, waving like some sociopathic drama teacher and before I know it, he and I are in the back seat of his car being driven back to Neutral Bay by his butler-manservant thing, in total silence.'

'Well, not a bad way to get about town. I imagine he requires a driver because he is in fact drunk for most of his waking hours.'

'I've been in his car before. It's quite impressive. Like something out of The Godfather, this huge black Rolls Royce thing. His driver never makes eye contact with anyone, not even him. He is this silent kind of robotic presence that just steers the wheel and breaks from time to time. Stephen never acknowledges him. I don't imagine they even speak, it's like he just has some homing device.'

'You've been to his house before, haven't you?'

'Yes. A few times. It's impressive.'

'That's a painful understatement. I've seen photos. It looks like Versailles if Liberace had designed it.'

'Well we walk in, and it's now pretty much pitch-black outside but the house is already lit up like a Christmas tree. He still isn't saying much so I am just following behind him, expecting to have him unhinge this thing, hand it to me and get back in his car and leave. But as we get to the room with the picture, this enormous sort of ballroom thing with mirrors and cream lounges everywhere, he just stands in front of it in silence.'

'What is the picture of again?'

'It's a Michael Zavros oil of that famous model as a Centaur.'

'A shirtless man? Shocking.'

'Well half a shirtless man.'

'For half a gay client. Works fabulously.'

'So, there I am just standing awkwardly behind Radley, watching him watch this picture and I'm saying nothing, just dying to be out of there.'

'Right. Well please tell me you just snatched it and ran out?'

'Trust me, I was going to.'

'But what? Don't tell me Veronica got in your fucking head about it? Darling she can't fire you for it. It's not your fault he didn't want to buy it. Let her deal with it.'

'I know. I know all that.'

'So, then what?'

'He turns to me finally and then says softly, What do you think?'

'About the painting?'

'Yes. Sort of shocked, I said, It's very nice. I said, It's a really interesting work. I said the artist is known for making comments on things like modern masculinity and male narcissism and this piece is a good example of that and that I would gladly have it in my own house. Which is all true of course. I didn't really know what else to say.'

'Hopefully he was already drunk enough that day to believe it all anyway.'

'So, he's nodding along, smiling at everything I'm saying, swaying slightly back and forth either from the alcohol in his system or just the sheer weight of his body buckling his knees, but whilst I'm talking something happens. Something about him, about the whole scene, this man and everything he was surrounded by; crystal chandeliers, taxidermy leopards, whole cabinets of ancient leather-bound manuscripts, Impressionist oil paintings. Beautiful important things. And he was utterly alone in it all. This great hulking mass. Stephen Radley the hobby art collector, the disappointing heir, the failed politician. Save for maybe a housekeeper, or the odd gardener that would come by, there would be no one else in his life. And I could see it in his eyes. He didn't care about the artist or the artwork, he was stalling. Asking these asinine questions over and over, just for the company.'

'Well darling I am sure he was wishing it was more than just an art history lesson.'

'It was clear to me that he was going to take whatever he could get. So, I just switched it on. Flirted my way through it. Charmed him into actually buying the damned thing and then walked off with a cheque.'

'And how did it feel?'

'Kind of empowering.'

'Good.'

'I guess it's just one of those things you see happen with girls in high school or in films or whatever, but I never knew was actually possible. People just flirting their way through something.'

'It's your body my love. Your youth.'

'Yes, it is.'

'Get some rest and we will chat tomorrow.'

* * * * *

'Are you awake darling?'

'Yes, I just got home from the bar. Is everything ok?'

'Yes. I think so. I mean, yes. I'm fine. Everything is fine.'

'What's wrong?'

'I wasn't completely honest with you before.'

'About what?'

'About selling the painting.'

'Which part?'

'Most of it was true. I didn't lie about selling it.'

'I wouldn't care if you did, as long as you're ok?'

'I was being smug. And I'm sorry.'

'Why are you apologising?'

'No, I was being smug because I didn't just flirt with Stephen Radley.'

'Ok.'

'It went further.'

'Right.'

'But it's not like that. He didn't force himself on me. It just kind of escalated.'

'Were you drunk?'

'No.'

'And he didn't try and manipulate or blackmail you or anything?'

'No nothing.'

'Did you want to do it then?'

'It's kind of hard to explain. In a way, I guess I did. But not because of any kind of attraction.'

'No, I imagine not.'

'I'm so fucking repulsed at myself. I have been lying in bed for three hours just staring at the ceiling. I have showered twice already also.'

'Can I ask what you did?'

'Everything.'

'Ok.'

'Fuck, it's disgusting, I know. That man. That man, that thing, naked and keeled over me, just heaving and breathing down onto my back. I can't believe it. I actually can't…'

'Darling, it's fine. Just be calm. I'm just trying to get to the bottom of this for you so I can help if you need me to. So, you weren't drunk and there was no force in this at all? Just making sure.'

'Yes.'

'Fine. Can I ask what made you go there?'

'Everything I said before was true. About seeing this lonely, pathetic man underneath all the money and influence. Some grotesque thing that could be exploited at a moment of vulnerability. What for him was pocket change. Tens of thousands of dollars, that he would not even realise had left his possession that night. Not lost a minute of sleep over. But for me, my first sale. Thousands in commission. A brief moment of success and achievement. So why not do it?'

'I get it.'

'And so, it started just at that. It started with the realisation that I could flirt my way to success. Stand there and grab his arm as I spoke. Laugh at his stupid comments. Touch him on the small of his back. Look him directly in the eyes as he talked at me, drunk, inane, ill-informed, unintelligent things into that vast opulent space. It started just as that. And I guess, once it had begun, I just didn't know how to stop it.'

'Ok.'

'I thought I had to see it through. I thought that if I was going to do this, I may as well do it right and ensure there is something at the fucking end of it all to walk away with.'

'Ok, darling I know you're probably feeling a bit confused and weird at the moment, but you haven't really done anything wrong.'

'Haven't I?'

'No. Based on what you said.'

'But what happens now? Every time he walks into that gallery, he is going to expect to fuck me first before he parts with any cash?'

'No. Of course not.'

'You know Veronica was there when I went back? Still. At 10:30 at night. Just sat at her desk, under a lamp. In complete darkness. I didn't say anything. Just planted the cheque on the table and looked down at her. She didn't even touch it, just glared at it. And without even making eye contact just turned back to her computer and said, Well done. Well done. Well fucking done. And immediately I could tell she knew. She fucking knew what I had done to get it. I bet she could still smell the sex on me as I stood there, completely dazed and absent. Fuck I feel fucking disgusting. I can't tell you how awful this feels.'

'She knew because she's inadvertently encouraged it. And I am certain she's probably done it herself too. The only reason she probably wasn't her laying under Stephen Radley's sweaty body tonight was because he's decided now he wants to fuck boys.'

'See. It never stops. This can't be the precedent for my career.'

'It won't be darling I promise.'

'I don't even want to think about it anymore. I'm sorry. I just came on to apologise, I'm sorry.'

'Darling don't go…'

'Goodnight.'

SATURDAY

'Y'know I was thinking about what happened to you last night…'

'Nothing happened to me.'

'Well I mean, yeah I know.'

'He didn't rape me.'

'I didn't say he did, but I don't think you were really in a position to say no.'

'Yes, I was. I could have taken that fucking picture off the wall and just walked out.'

'Ok…'

'I'm sorry I lied to you.'

'You didn't lie.'

'I didn't tell the truth.'

'I think you might have just been a little confused by what had happened.'

'I just need to clear my head a bit. I am going to go exercise. I will go for a swim.'

'Ok. Let's chat a bit later then.'

* * * * *

'How are you feeling now?'

'Better my love. Much better.'

'Any new on your pool boy?'

'So, his name is James.'

'We have a name!'

'Yes, seems so.'

'And how did this come about?'

'We walked out of the pool together tonight and stood in the park chatting coherently like normal people for a moment.'

'Thank Christ. What else?'

'He's from Manly.'

'Oh darling, across the bridge? May as well cut it off now. Long distances never work.'

'But he lives in Rushcutters Bay now.'

'That's better.'

'Turns out he is actually quite charming. Still completely reserved and giving so very little away. I dug just for these minor details. Still asked nothing of me.'

'She's married. I bet you there is a wife.'

'I'm not so certain. I think he's either just quite new to it all or incredibly shy.'

'New? You said she was 40.'

'I mean at this. Meeting guys and so forth.'

'Ok.'

'And that age, is also still to be confirmed.'

'Fine, well then what else did you find out?'

'That was it for today.'

'But was this preceded by your usual 40-minute shower session?'

'Of course.'

'I am living for the day when your grandchildren turn to you both and ask you how you met.'

'It's an easily avoided situation. We just won't have any.'

'Again, another exercising in polishing off the grime of the gutters we are forced to dwell in to present it back to the people who placed us there. How did you actually come across this as a cruise joint though? Did someone tell you? I'd never heard about it until you told me.'

'It was about two years ago, an ex-boyfriend of mine used to teach adult swim classes there. I'd wait for him to finish and we would go to dinner or lunch or whatever. Sometimes if he was late, I'd have a swim or just sit in the cafe. But one day I think I might have just caught the pool at cruise-'o'clock and there I was in the showers, minding my own business and suddenly, every cubical was occupied by some horny queer, rock hard in their speedos under the shower.'

'But I imagine you need to be careful no?'

'It's all a delicate little ballet. Despite it being flooded with gays, you always run the risk of finding yourself opposite some poor straight man who is legitimately there to use the change rooms. You have to assume the worst with everyone, despite how obvious it may seem. So, you walk into the showers, pretending you are only there to shower…'

'Which I imagine no one is?'

'Well, remains to be seen doesn't it?'

'And if they're not?'

'Well honestly they should be flattered regardless.'

'And is this how it all worked out with your pool boy?'

'James.'

'Yes.'

'We seemed to just always be there at the same time each day and then we developed this little routine after a while.'

'And now look at you.'

'But I don't have his number or anything, I don't even know if he's going to be there the time after I see him last.'

'Such is the life of a closet.'

'I don't know if he's a total closet. I think he's just a little hesitant maybe.'

'So, what now?'

'I wait for the next two pieces of the puzzle to fall out of his mouth. Hopefully that is tomorrow.'

'Hopefully.'

* * * * *

'How was Brunch?'

'I'm drunk.'

'Congratulations. I imagine that is Stella's doing?'

'Mostly, yes.'

'And so?'

'Well I'm drunk, aren't I? Mission accomplished as far as I am concerned.'

'I guess so. And your mother?'

'Fine as usual. Something was a little off with her though, I still can't quite put my finger on it.'

'Was she hung over?'

'One must always assume she is, but no I don't think it was that.'

'What did you two talk about?'

'Well, it started as it always does; I walk in and there she is forever early, forever ready, sat poised like a cat with its back arched. All that nervous, terrifying energy corseted in tightly under the corporate glamour. A certain kind of chaos doused in Bulgari eau du parfum and cinched in by a grey flannel pant suit and a YSL belt, to mask any trace of it.'

'A vision.'

'She doesn't realise I've arrived until I am standing over her, watching her smashing away at the buttons of her phone. She was there, completely alone in the whole fucking place. We went to The Winery on Crown Street, which I have never seen any less than completely full, bustling with yuppies and escorts. And there she was, sort of tucked away into a booth on the ground floor. It was so early in the day I don't even think they had the lights on because that blazing bright morning sun was illuminating everything anyway. Mother, I say as always through gritted teeth and a sort of manic smile (as I know she despises it when I call her by her actual name) and plant two breathy kisses on either cheek that barely connect to her heavily powdered face. And then the pantomime begins.'

'I'm dying to see this in action one day.'

'She starts with University, which usually lasts about a drink. She asks me which subjects I'm doing. Again. If I'm failing or not, which is of course her way of asking how I am going. Second drink comes and she asks me how my money situation is. Which I always say is fine, because I can't bear to get into a financial discussion…'

'I really do think she would be open to probably supporting you a bit, if you only asked. Just a bit of a top up here and there darling.'

'Absolutely not. Nothing that comes from her would ever be without strings. There is never a kind gesture bestowed upon anyone that is not wholly for her own benefit. Even money she can part with without feeling the most minute pinch in her own circumstance, she would expect complete and total control.'

'Like a loan?'

'No. She doesn't ever need it back. But she will require access to you if she is going to be funding you. Bank details, statements, further descriptions of outgoings and overheads. Debt history.'

'Well I guess that's only fair for her to want to know what her money is going to be spent on. Making sure you're not pissing it up against the wall.'

'No, it's a shaming exercise. It's to get access to your details and then sit back, feeling smug that you are the fucking deadbeat, artistic, flaky, queer offspring she always knew you were.'

'Ok then.'

'Trust me it's not worth it. Anyway, the money conversation is usually a two-drink conversation, because it's preceded by a tirade of the current state of affairs and her (I guess fairly informed but nonetheless arrogant) predictions for the country in the coming weeks. How much it will be fucked in the ass should Kevin Rudd actually succeed in toppling John Howard's government after all these years. How much the Labour party has turned into an anarchic group of left-wing, psychotic environmentalist's hell bent on destroying the very fabric of capitalist society.'

'That sounds like it might be a three-drink chat.'

'Well I usually just let her carry on through the food and then I'll peel off. She grabs the cheque; I make no attempt to even offer to pay. And that's us for a month.'

'So, it's all been fairly routine so far, by the sound of it?'

'Yes, but just as she is about to tuck into her steak tartare, without even looking up, she goes, So are you seeing anyone at the moment? Like it was some passing comment about the fucking weather.'

'I think I just spat out some coffee on the screen.'

'I was lucky to not have choked on the fucking mouthful of waffles I just took in myself, but there you go.'

'Where do you think that came from?

'Y'know I have always kind of knew this moment was coming. This sort of deathbed repentance thing that awful parent's get when they are confronted with their own mortality all of a sudden. That they need to make amends with their offspring to either assure their last moments in life are comfortable and guilt free. Maybe she is sick. Maybe she is finally seeing that this whole attempt to stage mother me into some over-achieving corporate closeted queer isn't working and her time is running out, so this is her attempt at starting to fain interest in me as a human and not as a commodity.'

'I don't think your mother is sick. I have a feeling she might have just run out of things to talk about, was feeling a bit loose after a bottle and a half of overpriced wine and sort of forgot who she was talking to?'

'Or that. Yes. Well regardless, I sat for a very brief moment and thought about giving her an answer that would move it along onto something else but then, I don't know, maybe it was the wine in me also, maybe I had just felt like shit stirring her a bit because I knew her guard was down. So, I told her.'

'About what? Darryl?'

'Yes darling. Our Darren. The Bankstown Stallion.'

'Christ. And how did that go down?'

'Well I just quite openly said, Well yes, Mother, funny you should mention it, I have just started seeing someone.'

'I'm sure she was the one choking on her waffles by then.'

'I have met someone, and HE and I have been out together a few times, HE's met some of my friends and I am going to see HIM again a little later tonight.'

'I see what you did there.'

'You should have seen her whole body just sort of melted down after it though. Her shoulders slouched forward, her spine kinked so that she was now slouched over her food slightly, she cocked her head and squinted at me briefly before smiling and then finally began to eat once again. Well that's nice, she finally said. And you think it would have ended there given her previous failings in being able to discuss homosexual relationships without a pursed set of lips. But then she carries on, And so what does he do?'

'Interesting.'

'And that was it. We were off. She was asking, I was answering. She probed and I provide matter to be probed. The more we spoke, the more she softened. She giggled her way through all the little bits I told her about us meeting and his car, and where he lives. Of course I was careful to omit certain details, least of which include his malfunctioning foreskin, but I was beyond candid with her and she was lapping it up.'

'Darling that's incredibly sweet, but I can't help but feel like there is more to this.'

'Nothing sweetheart, that was it.'

'Why do you seem so agitated by it though?'

'You can tell I'm agitated by what I am typing?

'Yes, I believe so.'

'No, I don't think so. I am a little tired though.'

'Really? You sure that's all?'

'I guess maybe I am just a little annoyed at the reaction she's had about me showing the prospect of a partner. This joy, albeit subdued by most standards but for Stella, it was as if she had suddenly broken out into song and dance.'

'I think it's sweet.'

'It is, but just some of the things she said around it. She said, more than once, that she is so glad I might be finally settling down.'

'Ok.'

'That I had maybe found someone to be with and so forth. How pleased she was at the prospect. It just seemed like such a backhanded comment.'

'Hmm, Stella struggles I think with pleasantries and I think maybe just being pleasant in general, so I wouldn't look too much into it darling. Again, probably the wine.'

'She just seemed so pleased that I wasn't running from person to person anymore. That I could *finally* start to build a life now…'

'This from someone who has just recently wrapped up her third attempt at a marriage?'

'It's such a fucking psycho hetero thing though, this constant, draining, energy sapping quest to find The One, isn't it?'

'Yes, but it's just hurled around so casually I think people don't really take it too seriously now.

'Don't they? I think people really don't take the time to unpick the damage it does to your outlook on life.'

'It's just a fantasy, but we need fantasy. Not everything can be so fucking literal, its rather boring.'

'But it's more so for those who claim to have found The One that I take issue, not the ones that are looking.'

'How so?'

'Well because they're kidding themselves massively into thinking that person is the person, they think they are. It's much more a case of, you'll do, than the universe has plucked you out of your circumstance and me out of mine and placed us together like some inexplicable miracle.'

'You don't believe in miracles anymore?'

'There's 7 billion people odd in the world and you've managed to secure The One that you just happened to find at your high school or some fucking shitty bar in your home town or in your case lurking in the change rooms of the Cook and Phillip Aquatic Centre.'

'If you are so wound up by this, why did you let her patronise you like that?'

'It was one of those things I didn't realise had happened until I left. Also, I kind of resent that sentiment though. Of finding some sort of relief in settling down with someone. That the idea of you sleeping around is concerning and a phase to be entered into quickly and exited just as quickly? Why can't we just keep sleeping around?'

'It's the heteros. They claim to have invented sex but then chastise each other for wanting it after marriage. Outside of marriage. After 40. After anything.'

'A rather odd lunch this one. But regardless I survived.'

'I wouldn't think too much of it darling. Your mother is softening as she ages it seems. There's going to be a lot more of these moment's where she thinks she is helping. She thinks she is offering good advice and being supportive. You just must give her the benefit of the doubt. Good intentions and all that. It's all we can do.'

'I am exhausted just considering it. And on that note, I will take a short nap and chat with you later.'

'Love you.'

* * * * *

'It just saw your text darling. A date! With the pool boy! That's fabulous. A real life, daylight date.'

'I wouldn't call it a date.'

'What would you call it?'

'I don't quite know. We essentially met naked, so what does one call that?'

'What will you do?'

'I think we are just going for coffee and see what happens after that.'

'In public?'

'So, it would seem.'

'Well good. This seems like some sort of step in some sort of direction. Whether or not it's the right one, let's wait and see. And what are you hoping to achieve from this? What objectives are we setting?'

'I like him.'

'Well yes. I gathered as much.'

'I like the way I feel when he is around. I get a nice vibe from him.'

'A vibe?'

'Yes. What else more can I go off?'

'Well don't ever discount the power of wondering how good of a fuck a guy might be, to completely override your rationale darling.'

'I am keeping an open mind.'

'I have no doubt that if he showed up on your door step tonight wanting to have sex, you'd be on all fours in seconds, but because he's dragging this out, for whatever reason, it's become this delicate little dance of flirting and seductive signals to string you along till the moment actually comes.'

'Yes, quite the opposite to simply logging on to BoyHunt or whatever the fuck it's called, firing off a couple of pictures of you spreading your ass checks in front of an IKEA mirror, leaving the front door open and hoping for the best.'

'Well regardless of what your intention is, I am very proud of you and wish you all the best with this supposedly handsome, wet, thing you have found. He sounds delicious.'

'Thank you.'

* * * * *

'Tracey is on the door tonight at 77, so we best get there before she finishes her shift.'

'It's a $5 cover charge. What does it matter?'

'Sorry I didn't know we were starting to burn our money.'

'I'm just saying.'

'Do as you wish.'

'I'm not going to have my night dictated by the shift of some girl you go to uni with and her willingness to, or not, let us in the club for free.'

'I'm going to be there at 11 regardless. In the line. Looking cute.'

'Are you though? Or will it be that black leotard under some jeans and a smoky eye again?'

'It's a brand.'

'Will Darryl be joining you tonight? How do you think he would handle the sights and sounds of Club 77?'

'No, actually he just left. And you best believe I am looking smug as hell right now…'

'Well you best hope your insides don't fall out when you're twirling about on the dance floor. Silly move bottoming before a night out darling. You should know better.'

'Well what was I supposed to do? He was in the area. And you were still at work, I was bored.'

'And hungry by the sounds of it.''

'Not anymore.'

'So, you're not going to disappear on me tonight then?'

'Nope. I'm all yours. He is going back to Bankstown as we speak. As far as I know…'

'Right…'

'I can tell I'm falling for him.'

'I was afraid you were about to say that.'

'I know he's problematic. But show me a queer who isn't?'

'Keep your wits about you my love. I've said my piece before, I don't want to repeat myself.'

'Send me a pic of what you're wearing.'

'Ok, one moment…'

SUNDAY

'So how long were we there for?'

'I think we left the club at 3am. And it's 7am now.'

'The glamour.'

'I won't sleep. I'm watching porn.'

'Me too. My cock is about as hard as a wet piece of sliced cheese right now, but there is something weirdly captivating about watching porn whilst you're high though. I become very forensic. Rewinding sections to examine them closer. Maybe I'm just enjoying the company.'

'What are you watching?'

'Something about a father teaching his son to light a campfire but he can't quite seem to find his matches without taking all his clothes off. How about you?'

'Something about a father teaching his son how to fix a car, but equally he can't seem to do it without fucking him first. I'll let you know how it ends.'

'What a fuss Tracey made tonight about kicking that poor boy out of her house. It just obliterated the mood, didn't it? Why would she make such a grand gesture insisting we all leave the club to go back to hers and then go and cause such a scene like that?'

'Preceded by yet another 6am, Mandy sponsored meltdown in front of everyone. She's become a bit of a late-night liability, this girlfriend of yours. All this crying and shouting all the time.'

'Yeah she's been rather unstable lately. I'd say Tracey was a mutual friend, no?'

'Mutual? No.'

'She's alright. Most of the time.'

'Yet again we end up back in that dilapidated, sparsely furnished terrace house on Palmers Street, with the creme del a creme of Darlinghurst. Just one heaving mass of torn black jeans, white singlets, eyeliner, stale cigarette smoke, halitosis and flat beer sprawled out on some once-was-beige, itchy and suspiciously crunchy carpet.'

'I know. Fabulous isn't it?'

'Nothing good happens after 3am in this city.'

'Yes but as gorgeous bright young things darling we must force ourselves through the motions to settle that nagging and persistent fear of possibly missing out on what might be the greatest party of our generation, and say yes to absolutely every invitation possible, no matter how sordid the crowd or late the evening.'

'Well as always with Tracey's little gatherings, the ratio of boys to desperate women is entirely tipped in the latter's direction.'

'Which ones?'

'I couldn't tell you their names.'

'I barely noticed a single woman there besides her. Then again, I rarely do.'

'Oh, they were there. Trust me.'

'Desperate for what exactly?'

'The tiniest whiff of male affection.'

'Well, water water everywhere…'

'Desperate for it in whatever form they can take it. Through whatever haze of booze and drugs they can handle it.'

'Then she shouldn't be kicking them out so freely. Who was he anyway? I assume she knew him vaguely?'

'No idea but c'mon darling, that whole scene she made about accusing him of stealing her drugs? Please…'

'I didn't think he did. I didn't see him move from that corner all night. He was right by my side the whole time.'

'Precisely.'

'Then why would she lash out at him in particular? Anyone there could have taken it. Or God-forbid, she was just too fucked to realise she racked the whole thing already.'

'It wasn't that darling. That poor boy was all over you all night. Touching your leg stroking your hair, laughing at everything stupid thing you said.'

'Yes, marvellous wasn't it? But alas, I resisted. My heart is elsewhere.'

'She didn't kick him out because she thought he stole her drugs. She kicked him out because he was competition.'

'I don't think Tracey is into fucking gay boys now, surely. As messed up as her sex life probably is.'

'No, it's got nothing to do with sex. She is part of that unfortunate collection of heterosexual women of this world who, for whatever reason, turn to the gays to feed their desire for male company.'

'Well, I mean, she could do a lot worse…'

'Really when you think about it, it's a match made in fucking heaven because all the ridiculous paradoxes of straight relationships are gone. Suddenly, men are no longer from Mars and we are all from Venus. We shop together, we flirt with boys, we watch the same TV shows and like the same music. All the dreams of finding their equal, their male partner who gets them and understands who they truly are, have momentarily come true. Except for one thing.'

'We don't fuck them.'

'Correct. And so, when we find ourselves a partner, and they are confronted with the idea of this perfect, albeit sexless, union fading away you watch how quickly they turn. So, seeing that cute little underfed art school drop-out fling himself at you tonight, is a very visual reminder of how fickle yours and hers relationship actually is. She is suddenly confronted with the risk of losing you to someone that would deem her automatically second fiddle should it ever eventuate.'

'I see.'

'And also, you spent the whole night languishing about, swooning over fucking Darryl, which I know didn't help the mood either. I watched her from my side of the room steaming like some love-sick wife being told in minute detail about the indiscretions of her dear husband.'

'I don't think Tracey of all people would care that much about Darren.'

'You watch darling, how her attitude changes as this progresses. Lord help us all if it does.'

'Thank you, darling that's very sweet.'

'And god forbid you are ever to try and present this behaviour back to them.'

'How do you mean?'

'Remember that time you actually uttered the words Fag Hag to those people outside the Taxi Club? She absolutely lost her mind.'

'She is though! And I have almost certainly heard her even say that about herself to other people.'

'It doesn't matter because the minute she hears you say it; it destroys the delusion she has about you both just being good friends doesn't it? Once you categorise it as that, which is what it is, you are peeling back the veneer of all the drinks and drugs and the 'Darrrrrling,' and the 'Babes,' and the 'This is my gay husband' and all that's she's left with is a boyfriend with a wandering eye and a penchant for cock. And that, I imagine, is quite a depressing realisation.'

'You've never liked Tracey.'

'Give me a reason to.'

'She harmless.'

'That's not a justification to be friends with someone.'

'She's fun.'

'She's an alcoholic.'

'No one can be considered an alcoholic before they're over 30. Until then, they're just party people.'

'You literally plucked her from behind a dumpster one night in ARQ and for some bizarre reason have not been able to shake her since. She worked at Best n' Less.'

'And now look at her.'

'Yes, quite. Running the guest list at 77 is a wild step up from scanning oversized, heavily discounted bras in East Gardens Plaza.'

'Something about her tonight did seem a little off.'

'I guarantee you it was that. And is that. Just keep an eye on it.'

'Well darling Tracey wasn't the only one tonight. Do you remember having a little episode outside Caratas House again, en route to 77?'

'Yes. Don't remind me.'

'Not the first time you've slumped yourself against the iron gates of that psych hospital in a stupor of vodka and Mandy.'

'I'm aware.'

'You just seemed rather fixated on what was going on inside this time.'

'I don't really know why but sometimes I think that with a head full of drugs and booze, wandering so aimlessly around those streets, how can we be so different to the people inside there?'

'Well the drugs and booze wears off eventually doesn't it? And, it's a choice to take it. I think very few if any people inside that place have chosen to be there…'

'I guess…'

'And show me a queer person with perfect mental health. We spend the first half of our adult lives lying through our teeth just to survive. It's not ideal.'

'At the very least, we become fantastic liars, don't we?'

'Some of the best.'

'I think I might need to rest finally now. The father has fixed the car. Both seem happy with the result.'

'You're not going to neck yourself on me, are you?'

'Perhaps. But I'll be sure to let you know just before I do so you can ensure I am arranged in an appropriately demure position when they find me.'

'It's Sunday and you're coming down. Don't think too much about it. Just have a sit-down shower. I feel it always helps. It's the closest I think you can get to feeling like you're being born again.'

'Right. I'll have to test that.'

'Get some rest and wake up fresh for your date with the pool boy.'

* * * * *

'Show me what you're wearing to this date that's not a date.'

'One second, let me turn my camera on.'

'Ok.'

'This.'

'Fabulous.'

'I will message you after x'

'Best of luck.'

MONDAY

'And so, what news have you of the outside world darling?'

'What are you on about?'

'I didn't hear from you after your date, so I decided to go twirling about without you. I can confirm that the boys, they missed you in Darlinghurst last night.'

'I highly doubt that. But how was it anyway?'

'Dazzling as always.'

'How you found the energy to show your face out after Saturday's efforts, I have no idea.'

'Oh, it was just meant to be a little dance at ARQ darling, nothing crazy. You know the Sunday nights there are always a bit lighter than the others. Skinny hairdressers and flamboyant retail assistants blowing off a bit of steam after having to work the weekend whilst we are all out rolling in the gutters. It's a fun crowd usually. Not the usual rough and tumble, shirts off, flex fest it is normally. The drag shows are at their finest on Sundays. Three in a row. Bang, Bang, Bang. On the hour, every hour. Tora Hymen, Prada Clutch. Vanity Fair. All the girls.'

'Who were you with?

'Tracey popped along with me. It was just the two of us. But she hadn't slept, bless her. She was a bit of a mess. Vomiting in the toilets at one stage. Probably shouldn't have been out on it again, but y'know how she is. She was on the Mandy again just to be able to function; I think. And mixing it with those awful black Smirnoff things. It wasn't pretty.'

'That's rather concerning.'

'Yes, I told her to leave, but I guess she was at that come down stage from Saturday of not wanting to be alone with her own thoughts and was just trying to power through. I was mostly ignoring her though, because Darren appeared eventually and so my attention was needed elsewhere.'

'Again, inside ARQ? Our Darryl?'

'Yes again. Totally on his own accord. Still with that rancid baseball cap on though. But arriving completely unchaperoned. And he would have needed to stand in that line and wait alone outside which I found rather impressive. Seems we are making some steps towards some progress....'

'Was he drunk?'

'Yes, I was just about to say he was actually incredibly drunk already when he showed up.'

'I imagine it takes quite a lot to get him like that, being the size he is.'

'In the beginning I thought it was doing him a world of good. You know a bit of Dutch courage and all that. Tracey had disappeared and was running in and out of the toilets on the ground floor, so Darren and I were leant against the bar, hands running up and down one another like a couple of high school kids, slipping me a sly kiss here and there, pulling me into his chest from time to time. All whilst the chaos of the world buzzed around us. It was adorable to see him so comfortable with it. So at ease with handing out affection outside the bedroom finally. He was wearing track pants can you believe. I could see the outline of his cock in his trousers growing like some python writhing inside a pillowcase. It was heaven.'

'Right.'

'It was bliss for a moment. Total bliss.'

'Only for a moment?'

'Well, just as midnight hits and the stage lights go on and Kitty Glitter appears to announce Tora's about to come on, I spin around to face the stage, as did everyone else there, and suddenly I feel this huge hand wrap itself around my arm and sort of yank me back. I turn to face him again and he has this look on his face like I'd just told him to go fuck his own mother and we just stare at each other for a moment before I ask him finally what the matter is. And then he starts…'

'What do you mean?'

'What the fuck is this? he says initially, gesturing behind us towards the stage. At first, I thought he was joking. We were inside a fucking gay bar and he's asking me what a drag queen is? So I think I giggled or something just as a bit of a knee-jerk reaction, but it seems to have made things slightly worse. I just kept looking from the queens on the stage back to him and watching his expression turn more and more from doe-eyed drunk to utter repulsion.'

'Was it that he seemed repulsed specifically at those drag queens?'

'No.'

'Just the image of a boy in a dress?'

'The idea, even the very thought of it, seems to have stirred something so vile down inside of him. I have never seen someone acting so outwardly disgusted before. So offended. He was actually causing a bit of a scene. Thank Christ none of the girls appeared to hear anything. I could tell the bartenders were listening though. I tried so hard to calm him down and slowly sort of edge him to the back of the club towards the pool tables, at the risk of causing a fucking riot in there.'

'To think someone thought they could waltz into a gay bar and garner some sort of sympathy from anyone else inside around being so fucking phobic towards drag queens?'

'I get this is all new to him. I was trying to be empathetic to what he was going through…'

'Don't you dare for a second make excuses for that darling.'

'I wasn't making excuses I was just trying to see where it might have been coming from.'

'That kind of behaviour is the very reason we fucking barricade ourselves inside these clubs. He needs to learn. And if he can't learn then he absolutely cannot have his cake and eat it too. He wants to fuck boys? He wants to creep around gay saunas? Well this is what it takes. What exactly did he say?'

'Disgusting, he just kept saying, To see a grown man act like that. So disgusting. He just repeated over and over. He said, For a man to dress not even like a woman but like a cartoon version of a woman was the most repulsive, unattractive thing and if they wanted to be women they should act like proper women. And men should be men. Act like men. How could anyone ever want to fuck a drag queen? And then finally, he says that the sole reason men become drag queens is because they probably have AIDS and no one will fuck them, so they turn themselves into the most unfuckable thing they can imagine.'

'Honestly?'

'Yes, really awful shit just pouring out his mouth.'

'It's disgusting. Please just cut ties with him immediately.'

'It was strange though. In amongst all this sort of still relatively contained mayhem, even in the dark of that club and the music and Kitty Glitter bellowing out over the sound system, after watching him flail about for a moment, I could tell he was overacting.'

'How do you mean?'

'Well there was a very real sort of repulsion obviously, in the things he was saying. Without a doubt. But the way he was saying them, it was so over the top. So theatrical, waving his hands about, gesturing wildly towards the stage, spinning around like he was about to storm off in disgust but then turning back again to continue. Like he wasn't just interested in making it known to only me that he was disturbed by it. But that anyone within ear shot and, had I not been there to calm it, probably the entire fucking bar. I mean here's this closeted thing that's crawled under his suburban fence and into the red lights of Oxford Street and suddenly he's in the belly of the monster face to face with Kitty Glitter's opening number.'

'And making it very known that although he enjoys sucking cock he absolutely does not approve of cross dressing. Because y'know, that's gay.'

'After about five minutes of this I had had enough, and I certainly wasn't going to be anywhere near him should Tora or Vanity catch even a word of what he was saying during their show. Being on the receiving end of a Queen's monologue even when it's light-hearted is brutal enough.'

'It would have done him the world of good to have experienced that. I wish you'd let him continue.'

'It was too much. I managed to somehow convince him to go outside for a smoke until he'd calmed down, but I think he was hesitant to leave without me for whatever reason.'

'And no one saw it or heard it?'

'Well if they did, they didn't make themselves known. I stayed and tried my best to enjoy the show. Tracey reappeared from the toilets, oblivious to the whole scene so she and I just continued to drink and flail about together. But I realised soon that it had been nearly two hours since I last saw Darren and was almost ready to give up thinking he had decided to take himself home finally, but as we were walking out to leave, I saw him emerge from one of the bus stops down the road. He seemed to have calmed down slightly but was still incredibly drunk I could tell. That huge body swaying about in the breeze, I could see from across the street. I sent Tracey on her way before I crossed over to see him and before I even stepped over the gutter, I could smell the chlorine fumes emanating from him. I knew he had been to Bodyline again.'

'Did you ask him?'

'Of course. And of course, he denied it. I didn't force the issue.'

'Again?'

'Yes again.'

'So did you shove him in a taxi and send him on his way?'

'No, he insisted on coming back home with me.'

'Why?'

'I have no idea. I thought the walk might do him good to sober up slightly so I all but carried him all the way down Bourke Street and slumped him in my bed. He fell asleep resting on my chest, completely dead to the world. That huge solid body curled up like a kitten. Full of so much fire and fury only a few hours ago, completely flaccid in my arms. He was gone by the time I woke up.'

'He was gone? Did you even hear him go?'

'No not really. I thought I dreamt something, but I can't really recall. It was like he wasn't even there. Like the whole thing didn't even happen.'

'I'm sure he remembers nothing darling, but I have no doubt that despite whatever state of booze induced impairment he was in, that those feelings dwell within him still in daylight hours also.'

'I know. I know. What sad heterosexual trauma do you think this poor boy has had to make him behave like this?'

'God only knows…'

'Well I'm sorry you had to deal with all this, but please do just cut this off immediately.'

'I'm curious about this though.'

'About specifically?'

'About his reaction specifically.'

'No one is born with this fear of queerness. It's learned.'

'I guess so.'

'It's beaten into people. By fathers and brothers. Mothers and sisters too. Women can be just as brutal. All it takes is for one fleeting moment of a parent walking down a street, holding their child's hand and passing a man who may be in trousers that are, say, a little too tight, a blouse that may look like it was pulled from the women's section of a sale rack in David Jones and a boot with a slightly too high heel. His hair may be blown out and up to some extraordinary height, he may be in lipstick that day because he was feeling particularly beautiful. His earrings might be heavy with rhinestones and twinkling in the morning sun as he passes them, mincing on his way. He might be a vision of beauty.

But the parent may scoff. Laugh a little, draw the child's eye to the person they are passing and point. They may attempt to illicit an innocent giggle from the child in that moment, as adults do, but at the expense of someone queer. And then suddenly that child, at the tender age it is, learns that faggots are the source of ridicule. Exactly as one is taught to laugh at a cartoon character slipping on a banana peel. But for what? What is so fucking funny? Nothing.'

'Surely, it can be unlearned then. We aren't laughing at people slipping on banana peels, now are we?'

'Well laughter turns to ridicule. And ridicule can be violent. Pushing the person you are making fun of so far down into the mud they are barely recognisable when you are finished with them. But I guess, yes, like all things, it can be unlearned. If one wishes to unlearn them. Have you heard from him yet this morning?'

'I have not.'

'As I said, he probably remembers nothing of it. Will you bring it up to him when you speak next?'

'I don't know.'

'If you have the energy to, I think you should.'

'I guess I just am suffering from that idiotic sense of hope that people, even people like him, can change.'

'You're giving him a very wide berth. I have no doubt that the sex is good, and you get off on the thrill of being with a closet, but is it all worth it?'

'I don't know my love. I really don't.'

* * * * *

'Oh, fuck darling, I'm so sorry, I didn't even ask you about your date with the pool boy! Sorry, sorry…'

'It's fine, you had an eventful evening.'

'No, I'm a cunt. Can you chat now? Shall I call?'

'Not really, but it's ok to talk on here. I am at the gallery but it's quiet. Shockingly.'

'Ok, great. Dish. Tell me.'

'It was actually amazing to be honest.'

'Brilliant. I love it.'

'Typically, I haven't stopped thinking about it. Just how easy it all felt. To talk to him after all this time of just glaring at him. It was quite intense.'

'Did you finally fuck?'

'Really?'

'What?'

'You know this is why you're still waking up under drunken straight men who are terrified of drag queens. You are so crude.'

'I'm only playing darling. Just fucking tell me, c'mon, I'm dying here.'

'We met at this tiny little wine bar in Rushcutters Bay, I can't remember what it was called. I don't think it even had a name. It was like someone just placed some bar stools into a corner shop, threw up a chalk board with double digit prices for fairly forgettable glasses of wines and called it a bar. But we had it to ourselves thankfully. Just us and this beautiful girl behind the counter, waiting on us the whole time. It was so peaceful.'

'Yes, I know the type.'

'He looked so painfully handsome too. And such a strange experience to be on a date with essentially a complete stranger, knowing already how he looked beneath his clothes. It sort of meant I could just focus on what he was saying.'

'And not spend the whole time trying to catch passing glances of the outline of his cock through his pants?'

'Something like that, yes. He was a little bit late but wasn't flustered. As soon as he appeared, I was sort of mentally preparing to have to manage all that nervousness that seemed to consume him when we were chatting at the pool, but he was completely and utterly calm. Just showed up in beige trousers, a tight black t-shirt and sandals, like he was going out to get a newspaper and a fucking latte. Like it was nothing.'

'What did you talk about?'

'I think we just started initially on about something innocuous like the pool and the people we both normally see. Those fat bankers with pink jowls and bellies so wide they can't even see their own dicks when they shower. The emaciated, nervous little gays that dart in and out of the change room all day whose skin turns translucent from hours of standing under the hot water. The straight men that appear to know nothing of it. The receptionists who know about it all but pretend not to. He knows because he sees it too.

He watches them like I do. This odd little microcosm of life and sex and attraction in that damp, airless room that ironically sits in the shadow of St. Mary's Cathedral.'

'Well I guess at that point in time it's what you both had most in common, yes?'

'It was just pleasantries initially, but after we ordered some drinks we moved on a little and he started telling me about his work. It seems he runs some sort of luxury imports business.'

'Very nice. Don't sign a prenup then.'

'Shut up.'

'What kind of imports?'

'I think things like furniture and antiques, mostly from Europe. It's a family business though, I didn't get the impression it's been some sort of life-long passion. He doesn't strike me as someone with a strong eye for design or art or history. As smart and as charismatic as he comes across.'

'Doing it for the money mostly?'

'Just the way he would respond when I probed him a bit on some of the objects, like this chandelier he was currently having brought into the country from an old chateau in the Loire Valley. He began to describe what it looked like and then sort of just trailed off, mumbling before glaring out the window into the distance. I didn't push it. I wasn't interested in making him feel stupid.'

'Well, I mean, he's a businessman. Just because he doesn't know the minute details of 17th Century French crystal, I don't think is cause for concern just yet.'

'Like I said I didn't push it. He mentioned also that he's married.'

'Right.'

'To a woman. And they have a child, a young one.'

'Heavens.'

'He told me quite early on too.'

'How did he even bring it up?'

'When I asked him where he lived, he said it almost in passing that it was nearby, with his wife and child. He very clearly wished I might have either not heard it at all, or that I would mention something similar so as to not draw attention to it.'

'And did you?'

'Well no, I don't think so. I just nodded and then told him how nice I thought it was that he was a father and so forth. Which I guess, is true. I let him finish also, because I didn't particularly want to talk too much about it but was happy to let him tell me as much as he was comfortable with. His wife doesn't work, they've been married since they were about 20 or so.'

'I see. He wasn't showing you pictures, or anything was he?'

'No, God no. But I can only imagine. She's probably some tall drink of water herself.'

'And what of the child?'

'She had apparently wanted one forever. The wife. But had some issues conceiving. So they went and did the IVF thing. And now they have this 9-month-old little girl. I didn't get the name. Possible he didn't say.'

'It's rather sweet but there's something so fucking tragic about it all isn't it?'

'About him?'

'About the fact that all this perfectly handsome, perfectly heterosexual couple wanted, needed, to make their lives even more handsome and more heterosexual was a child and finally they got one and he celebrates by going cruising for boys at the local aquatic centre.'

'I didn't say he wanted it. I said she did.'

'It's kind of beside the point really. Do you think she knows he's gay?'

'I'm still not entirely sure he thinks he's gay. But I also didn't get the impression there was any kind of open agreement between them.'

'Sort of turns a blind eye because she wanted the baby more than she cared about him.'

'Quite possibly.'

'This is all a bit much.'

'It weirdly didn't seem so when I was talking to him about it directly. You have such a talent for making things seem so sleazy though, thank you.'

'Honey, of course you weren't turned off by this. You've been head over heels for this man since you laid eyes on him. He could have told you he had 16 wives and 40 children, and you'd probably still be drooling over him.'

'I doubt that. It just seemed like he had done quite well to compartmentalise that as one part of his life and then there was the other part.'

'The pool?'

'Well the pool and everything it represents. Time alone, away from his family. To be as he wishes to be. We didn't talk much about it.'

'I imagine you didn't.'

'We sat there for a while, getting slowly pissed on the forgettable wine, sweating in the afternoon sun beaming through those filthy bay windows. Strangely neither of us were hungry or even motioned towards having dinner. I am not even sure it was on the cards. So, when we stood up to settle everything, we just ended up loitering on the corner talking shit for a minute. Then finally he says to me he has some more wine back at his house if I cared to join…'

'YES.'

'Turns out he lived just across the street.'

'That's ah, rather brazen of him?'

'Yeah I thought so too. But I was tipsy, so it seemed more convenient than anything at the time. We walked into this small but beautifully renovated, two story terrace house that had had the entire back wall ripped off and replaced with a glass atrium and opened into an intricately manicured Japanese style garden. It was so modern and slick, maybe one or two antique pieces about. I spotted an enormous sort of Georgian gold mirror in the hallway as we walked in and then this blue and white Chinoiseries vase in the kitchen bench, but that was about it. Everything else looked like it had been bought the week before. Concrete, chrome, black leather. Stylish but austere. Certainly not the kind of place you'd expect a dealer of all things ancient and beautiful to live. But there you go.'

'Maybe his wife wears the decorating pants and she prefers the more masculine aesthetic. Possibly all they have in common now?'

'We didn't even get to this wine he supposedly had. Once we were inside and he had made certain the coast was clear, he turned to me, pulled me against his body and we began kissing.'

'God, I love this.'

'It was intense.'

'Sort of concerning that he had to make sure the coast was clear only once you were inside. Kind of kinky if he thought his wife might have been there?'

'She was apparently out of the state with her mother and the baby. He was checking for the cleaner.'

'Ah, very good. Then what happened?'

'We didn't fuck in their bed if that's what you're wondering. I don't think he was interested, and I probably would have suggested otherwise. So, we kept it to the couch. And it was perfect. I can't put into words how perfect it was. There is something so serene about such a large man being so gentle. So careful and measured with how he moves about your body and how he touches you. A softness without being hesitant or nervous. He sort of had me pinned down at the start with these giant hands pressing my own above my head. Not aggressively, but just holding me in position as he kissed and gently ran his tongue up and down the area just beneath my jaw and then up to my ear lobes, over my chest and just softly over my arm pit. He didn't even touch my cock for the first fifteen minutes. I was writhing in agony over how good it felt and wanting him to just grab it and jerk me off till I came then and there, but I think he was getting off on the temptation. By the time he got to my stomach with his tongue, his cock was completely wet, sliding around on my thighs as he moved further and further down my body. Even when he was all the way there, he still managed to hold my hands up above my head somehow, not letting me touch myself at all, just totally relinquishing every bit of pleasure to him.'

'Seems he knew what he was doing then?'

'I have no doubt. It was like months of pent up sexual energy just all boiling to the surface. But not exploding in some messy sort of eruption, just like a slowly overflowing sink. He must have rimmed me for at least ten minutes, nonstop. Just slowly. So slowly. I feel like I spent nearly an hour on my back also just staring up at him as he slid his cock in and out of me. Laying there, looking at this great marble slab of a man being so gentle with my body.'

'Amazing.'

'When it was all done we just lay there on the couch, naked and wet with sex and sweat, our hearts thumping through our ribs from the exercise, watching the last peek of sun turn the sky red, purple and then dark blue, through the glass box of his back garden.'

'Did you stay the night?'

'No, no. But I did fall asleep eventually, just wrapped around him. I can't say for how long. But when I woke up, he wasn't with me. It took me a moment to orientate myself obviously, but I caught him at the end of the couch, still naked, just staring out into the darkness of his garden. Not saying anything.'

'That's slightly strange…'

'As I was watching him, I heard him sniffing a few times, like he might have been sobbing or something and sat up quickly ready to rush over, but then I realised he was smoking, so must have just been the cigarette.'

'I see.'

'He didn't turn around for a while, so I just laid back down watching his beautiful shoulders rise and fall with the drags he was taking, basking in the memory of what we had just been doing. But when he noticed I was awake eventually he flicked his smoke out the door and slid back towards me, smiling. Asked me if I had a nice nap and if I wanted anything to drink or eat. It must have been almost midnight and as much as I would have stayed on the couch for the rest of my queer life, I knew that it was probably my cue to leave. So, I politely declined and gathered my things to go.'

'How gorgeous. All this. And so what now?'

'Well it's 10am, so it's been officially 10 hours now since I saw him. I imagine I should probably leave it a little while longer before I go knocking on his door again. What do you think?'

'If it were me, I wouldn't have left.'

'I am finishing here at 1pm, shall we head to the beach? I think I need a swim.'

'Yes, fabulous idea.'

* * * * *

'Christ, wait till you see this…'

'What?'

'Let me copy and paste it, one second. You'll die.

Hello Love,

I hope you're all good. Your father, sister and I are going to be coming to the city on Thursday to watch the Rugby at the SF Stadium. We are all staying together at the Travelodge on Wentworth Street just

*for the night. We have a ticket for you to join, we'd
love for you to come. Or at least a dinner if you like.
Maybe you could invite your friend also? The one
from Uni?*

Lots of love,

Mum x.'

'God that's adorable. Hilarious but adorable.'

'Is it though?'

'Yes.'

'Why would she think I'd enjoy doing that?'

'Oh, don't be so miserable.'

'Have you ever even been to one of these things?'

'A Rugby game?'

'Yes.'

'I don't think I have, no.'

'It's like something out of fucking Gladiator. A
stadium packed with thousands of drunk screaming

spectators glaring down at a couple of over gown men, essentially bashing each other for 90 minutes.'

'I am strangely aroused.'

'It's far from arousing.'

'She's reaching out to you to connect. It's the exact same thing you told me Stella was trying to do at brunch on the weekend. Albeit in a much more ah, grass roots sort of way, shall we say?'

'I guess.'

'And she did give you an out, just to go to dinner.'

'She already has a ticket.'

'Well it's only Monday darling, you have a few days to decide.'

'I honestly would rather not.'

'Just, go, shout, get drunk, hang out with your sister. Smile. Play happy families. They love you.'

'I think they love an image of me. I just seem to complete the collection when we are all together, but I know they'll secretly be anxious about what I might wear or what I might say. How I might act.'

'Ok, I get it.'

'I hate painting them in a negative light. I do. Because they're good people. I just don't think they've really figured out how to manage this quite yet.'

'Maybe don't think about it yet. I am sure you can let her know later when you've figured out what you have the energy to do.'

'Yes, I will.'

'Did you get home from the beach ok? Christ it was hot today.'

'Yes, I really do hate that journey home though. It's disgusting.'

'Isn't it just?'

'Cramming ourselves onto those overstocked buses of steaming hot bodies, all still dusted with sand and slippery with oily sun cream. Like fucking chickens on some dilapidated truck heading to the abattoir.'

'One day we will have cars darling. Like all the rich school boys of Vaucluse and Dover Heights with their roofs down and polished hubcaps glistening in the sun. One day.'

'One day.'

'An interesting choice of beach today as well my love. Of all the little spots we could have gone to.'

'You have never been to Lady Jane beach before?'

'No, I think I would remember if I had.'

'It really is one of the most stunning beaches in the whole city.'

'You could have told me it was nude.'

'What does it matter, we are virtually nude at a beach anyway?'

'Yes, I know, but it really is something you should probably prepare for, before going. Mentally and I guess physically.'

'You saw the guys there though darling, most of them could give less of shit.'

'Because most of them were over the age of 60.'

'And didn't they look fabulous?'

'I ah...'

'It's true that body confidence belongs not to those who have achieved some kind of hyper-aesthetic, but to those who have lost the desire to care what others think.'

'I think that comes with age.'

'I think it comes with the realisation that body perfection is wholly unachievable.'

'Whilst we are waiting for this realisation though, do we continue to try and look beautiful?'

'Of course, we do.'

'Noted.'

'I have to admit you were a little distant this afternoon.'

'I was?'

'Yes.'

'I'm sorry I didn't mean to be.'

'Were you still mulling over what happened with Radley?'

'I guess in a way.'

'Did you want to talk about it?'
'I'm ok, I think I was just sort of trying to rationalise it against what happened with James last night. Something so awful versus something so beautiful. All in the space of a few days.'

'Ok.'

'I'm trying so hard to be level-headed about him.'

'About your pool man?'

'Yes. But I can feel this burning obsession about it all really starting to grow quite rapidly.'

'That's sweet.'

'I don't ever stop thinking about him. Even before we met. I would walk into that fucking place sick with excitement at the thought of even seeing him. Because so often I would. So often that excitement was appeased by the sight of him there; wet, naked, smiling. The smell of that pool instantly makes me think of him. Any pool really. I can't even walk past it without slipping into some daydream, about him.

'It's nice darling. It's sweet to hear you talk like this.'

'I'm sorry, I hope I didn't mean to be so absent.'

'Have you heard from him yet then?'

'No.'

'And you've reached out?'

'I have only once. Just a text. A thinly veiled check in and thanks for his hospitality with of course a strategic, seemingly innocuous question at the end to try and incite a response.'

'Very cunning.'

'But it's taking every ounce of my strength not to send him a barrage of others. I just can't stop thinking about him.'

'I know darling. It's equal parts very sweet and wildly pathetic you falling in love with this married man. But I get it. I do. He's gotten to you.'

'I'm setting myself up for a huge heartache here aren't I?'

'Well no, not necessarily. You may have caught him on the precipice of a massive leap he could be about to take into a new fabulous life.'

'But should I be wanting to be the reason that a man, a husband, leaves his family.'

'That's a fucking dumb thing to say.'

'How? Who wants to be a home wrecker?'

'That! That right there.'

'It's true.'

'No darling. You didn't force him to fuck you. You didn't force him to take you on a date. You didn't force him to cruise you for months on end at that pool. He chose to do that.'

'Maybe.'

'He's clearly queer in some way, shape or form. You've just been the vehicle for that manifesting. If he leaves his family to be with you or even leaves his family because of you, it's not your problem.'

'I don't want that hanging over me though.'

'Home wreckers are bimbos from the suburbs who get taken on fancy dinners by awful men who work in finance and are convinced they've hopped on some gravy train but can't handle it when they go back to their wives. That's when the home wrecking starts. This is different.'

'It no less of a mind fuck.'

'Are you feeling jealous? Of his situation? The wife etc.'

'Of course, I fucking am.'

'Ok.'

'That she gets to roll over and watch him still sleeping in the morning. That he probably still kisses her at night even though he is thinking about someone else.'

'You?'

'Anyone. Just someone else. That he's probably tried to tell her he is struggling, hurting even, but she's too focused on keeping their vision of a family together, she won't address it. I am jealous that she has his time when I know, I can see, he longs to be elsewhere.'

'I'm sorry darling…'

'It's fine. I think I'm just a bit exhausted by it all. I should have an early night.'

'Good idea.'

'Let me know if you hear from him in the meantime.'

'I will.'

'Love you.'

'oxo'

TUESDAY

'Do you ever think that John Howard was ever attractive?'

'Who?'

'John Howard darling. The Prime Minister of Australia?'

'Oh. Her. Ah, no. I do not.'

'Sometimes there are some angles I see of him when he is in one of these TV debates that I think maybe there might have been a few years when he had hair, maybe a bit leaner, like a private school rower or something, in those tiny white shorts, where he might have been.'

'I have a feeling that they only allow unattractive white men into the parliament of this country. It's like a prerequisite to step into any kind of leadership role in Australian Politics.'

'It's a shame really. Politics needn't be so grim. Even the wives of these men don't really seem to relish much in the spotlight. Where are our Jackie Kennedy's?'

'I think there is always an expectation that glamour has no place there.'

'I think that's sexist.'

'How?'

'Well considering it has been and continues to be mostly men running this country, it would be men that have set that standard. That only people in dull, gun-metal grey, ill-fitting, polyester suits have the capacity to run the county effectively. When has anyone in something even slightly more than that ever been given the chance?'

'Not to my knowledge. Anyway, what's Mrs Howard saying today that's got you so curious?'

'Well he's on ABC debating Kevin Rudd on the Kyoto Protocol.'

'The what?'

'The Kyoto Protocol. It's a UN convention that tries to hold countries to account for their greenhouse gas emissions and commits them to reducing it.'

'I see. And how is it working?'

'Well, that's what they're debating. Howard doesn't seem to be too fond of it.'

'And what of Mr Rudd?'

'Very keen to work on it.'

'Isn't it all rather dull darling to listen to these old men blabber on about this stuff?'

'I think this man, this Rudd man, leader of the opposition as they say, will finally be the downfall of this awful fucking government. Ten years is far too long for a leader of a democracy to be in power. Ten fucking years. Kick them out after 8 like the Americans do, I say. And I'm not ageist, but I just don't believe someone who was educated in the 1940's and 50's really could possibly know what is best for a country in 2007.'

'Mother Stella seems to think he's one of the greatest leaders this country has ever had.'

'She would.'

'Your parent's too, I imagine.'

'Christ don't remind me. Stella seems to have at least some sort of informed opinion about it all. Regardless if I agree or not. My parents on the other hand, tend to just paraphrase headlines of the Daily Telegraph and use them as seemingly convincing anecdotes when pressed about their opinions.'

'Well you seem to have come out of that rather unscathed then?'

'With my peasant education?'

'I didn't say that.'

'You meant it.'

'Oh, shut up.'

'I'm kidding darling.'

'Fuck off would you.'

'Sweetheart, you needn't be so ashamed of your beautiful schooling in one of the state's BEST schools. All the money Stella could afford.'

'Expensive private schools don't always mean a better education. Some of the biggest drug dealers I know, came out of the private school system of this state.'

'Yes, I can attest to that. Money well spent I say.'

'And it doesn't mean that people come out of it more informed either. Some real conservative fucking cunts are running that school and guess what they produce?'

'More conservative cunts.'

'Precisely.'

'So why pay it then?'

'Because people will always consider money to equal quality. But there isn't any private school for teachers. These teachers are all coming out of the same universities with the same qualifications. A shit teacher is still going to be shit if they're at a private school or a public school. Throw an Olympic sized swimming pool, a few laptops for the students and a tie and blazer and people are convinced their kids are learning better than the kids down the road in sweaty fibro sheds with malfunctioning ceiling fans and 2b pencils. It's just not true.'

'Well they deserve to lose their money then if they're being so ignorant about it.'

'For all your parents' supposed failings in their political leanings, I believe they did the best job they could have possibly done at the time, in raising you. I think public school boys are hotter anyway.'

'Oh god. Darling no. I don't know what kind of distorted fantasy you have of the boys I went to school with, but no. You went to school with a bunch of beefed up rugby players in suits who drove Range Rovers. How could you possibly even think about anything else?'

'The grass is always greener isn't it?'

'It wasn't. Though I will say it had its moments.'

'Tell me…'

'Christ, here we go.'

'What?'

'You. Wanting me to fulfil your sick poverty-porn fantasy of hot boys from council estates getting boners in class and pulling each other's shorts down on sports fields.'

'Well, if you're offering.'

'It was dangerous. There were moments of excitement here and there but all in all it was really quite a dangerous time to be fooling around with boys.'

'Didn't that make it kind of sexy though?'

'No of course it didn't. It's not the sort of excitement you feel sucking a guy off in a bush at some family picnic grounds, the repercussions of which are merely a few red-faced parent's and a hastily packed away spread of salads. The repercussions of this were everyone at school and in the immediate surrounding areas, finding out that irreversible claim of being a faggot. And in a school that was basically like a day-care for delinquents, it was out of the question. I watched boys beat one another into a bloody pulp over nothing more than a sideways glance. What do you think they would have done if they came to school one day and found out I was gay?'

'How did you get away with any of it then? Why would you even risk doing anything with a guy if it was that bad?'

'I don't know. I honestly don't know.'

'Must have been quite the temptation then.'

'There were always these parties. House parties. Usually the children of absent parents who had an older sibling that was kind of in on the action. We would place an order of booze with them on the Wednesday or Thursday, bring tiny wads of cash to school, hand them to whoever's brother or sister was buying it and then arrive the night of to a dining table of glistening bottles of cheap tequila, cardboard cases of warm beer, sparkling wine and packets of Winfield Sky Blue cigarettes. And then that would be it. 16

years of age, our tolerance was non-existent and all we needed was the aforementioned supplies and we had a party. Nothing else.

No one could go home. Everyone had to spend the night, at the risk of facing their own parents drunk. So we would collapse in a chair, on a lounge, under a table. Side by side like some very poorly run army barracks. And I guess that would be it. I'd find myself lying, almost comatose next to some curious boy I barely speak to in class, but who's hand you suddenly find sat heavily on the front of your boxer shorts. And the touching would begin. Never a kiss, never anything that would be considered sex. Just curious touches, jerking. Exploring. Cumming together. No talking, no connection. It never even really occurred to me that these guys might be gay or even bi. They were just reaching out into the darkness for anything to help them do whatever they felt like in their drunken state. And of course, there I was.'

'But there you were also slowly falling in love night after night with these drunken souls thinking they might have singled you out specifically. That'd you'd found another unicorn in a pack of donkeys.'

'I guess maybe the first few times, I thought so. That I'd found another person who was like me in that cesspit of a school. But it didn't take long to realise it wasn't so. During the daylight hours that would follow, this kind of heavy, quite aggressive silence would form between me and whoever had reached out that night. I could tell that should I ever consider vocalising what had happened between us to anyone, my life would not be worth living. I understood that these moments of what I saw as albeit brief but early, innocent passions, were for them a crippling source of embarrassment and anxiety. And then there's every other boy your age coming to school after the weekend gloating about the poor girls they've just spent all of the Friday night before poking and prodding with their dirty fingers and pimply lips and you have to sit there, silent, pretending like you didn't give their friend a hand job in the next room. I see these boys now still when I go home to visit my family. Some are married. Some have kids. Some even have fairly decent jobs. I see them in the street and for a moment, they look at me like every other stranger passing until it hits them; I am the person that caused them to have maybe their first and maybe still their only, sexual experience with another man. Then it spreads across their faces. This fear. That I hold the secret that they feel could crack the entire foundation of their beautiful hetero lives with some simple, innocent story. Of such an inconsequential thing. But such is the fragility of Australian masculinity. That. That is what you carry around with you if you were fooling around with boys at that high school.'

'I see.'

'And that is what we carry around with us forever. The shame. That the first impressions we have of our sexual experiences are not sources of pride and juvenile smugness or of relief and excitement. But shame. Shame and fear. That we have acted on some impulse that could get us beaten up, bullied into isolation, kicked out of home, entirely ostracised beyond help. And on top of that, we must deal also with the responsibility and guilt that we have partaken in some activity that the other person may regret instantly. That the minute that cum leaves his cock, immediately realises that he didn't enjoy it and wishes to forget it. That you will forever be seen as some queer predator that coerced them into it. And what recourse have you got for denying what happened in that room that night? Nothing. Queers are always on the back foot. Always painted as sexual deviants, hell bent on converting every straight man they come into contact with.'

'And you can tell no one.'

'You can't and won't tell a soul for years to come. So, let that pour over the already festering mound of generic stress and anxiety that all teenagers have, and you might have some fragment of understanding what it would be like to fool around with boys at that high school.'

'It's suddenly become a lot less sexy.'

'It's because it wasn't. I mean how different could it have possibly been for you though?'

'Darling, you forget that I was rather a late bloomer. I was celibate until only two years ago. I am fresh as a daisy.'

'Yes, well unfortunately it seems that daisy has imploded into a rosebud now I imagine.'

'The private schooled, catholic, picture of perfection. I even had girlfriends. But I made sure they were as disinterested in consummating the relationship as I was. And so, I think I just avoided it. I don't know if it was a subconscious thing because I was too scared to even try. But of course, it was all smoke and mirrors. And then once school was done. Well, as you say. The implosion began.'

'And poor Stella, meeting all these pure, virginal little private school girls thinking she was going to have some sort of stable family unit after all, and then there you go.'

'Oh please. You think she was ever home enough or sober enough to meet them? It was for my own benefit only. I think about them often actually. These girls. There weren't many. Only three. Casey Mason, Jasmine Mitchell and Rayleigh Adams. All brunettes.

All pure and pious as the day is long. Bless them. I imagine I, now the whole school must surely realise that I am out, must be a blight on their histories as well. Straight women do tend to carry around this strange burden of feeling like they are responsible for turning a partner gay. But whatever, let them think that. It's funny. Let them think they have that ridiculous superpower if they wish.'

'Poor Stella.'

'And what of your parents?'

'I had no girlfriends to speak of. I never brought home anyone.'

'Oh, and have you decided whether or not you will see them?'

'Of course, I will see them. I just am not sure where and at what point.'

'At the Rugby?'

'I don't want to think about it.'

'HA! Darling though, surely when they do those change room shots during the halftime bit or whatever it is, as brief as they are, they make up for it.'

'I mean yes, but I have to pretend not to notice, don't I? Imagine if they streamed that live directly onto the screens at ARQ? There'd be a fucking riot. But no, in a stadium of straights, everyone just watches and nods along, like the packages of 24 of the hottest men in the country aren't glaring down at them from a 60ft screen.'

'Why do they always strip off during those bits? Like does it help them to listen to what their coach is saying if they're naked? We aren't complaining though. Fuck if giving each other rim jobs helps them to focus, I'm all for it.'

'Agreed.'

'God, I love your parents so much, they are so adorable.'

'You're not coming.'

'Why not?'

'Because you weren't invited.'

'Yes, I was!'

'She didn't mean it.'

'Every time I see them, they are always so insistent on me joining next time. I think I should just come along.'

'I don't think the world of professional football is ready for you. And anyway, you will just spend your whole time at the urinals anyway.'

'This is most likely true. What about dinner?'

'No.'

'Why not?!'

'Because darling, I cannot stand the way they fawn over you and your mannerisms. It's like they are inadvertently trying to say, We accept you, to me, through you. They won't ask me about anything, but will laugh and clap along to you talking about blow jobs in alley ways with men you met at work.'

'That's a shame. So you won't bring up James to them?'

'They won't ask. And no, how could I expect them to be even remotely sympathetic towards falling for someone with his circumstances.

'Darren actually messaged me today, planning something for this evening. How is that? Not just appearing out of the shadows anymore. Says he wants to meet tonight at my place. I said I was busy until after 10 with your gallery opening, but I think I will duck off after if that's ok?'

'It's fine my love. You really don't need to come if you have plans. It'll be dull as always.'

'Of course I will be there darling. As much to support your fine work putting it on as is it to drink Veronica's overpriced bar dry.'

'Come. Drink, Be obnoxious.'

'I think I just may. Besides my legs, what else is being opened this evening?'

'It's a rather dreary collection of about 80 prints by Goya called The Disasters of War. Ranging in price from $2,500 up to $10,000 apiece.'

'Yes, I know the work.'

'Should be a decent crowd. Names like Goya always tend to give rich people erections.'

'She shouldn't be splitting them up though. They were made as a set to be seen all together, those things.'

'I know darling, but finding one person to spend upwards of half a million dollars in one hit is much less likely than getting numerous people to part with significantly less, isn't it?'

'She is so vile. It's like you're working at the McDonald's of the art world.'

* * * * *

'Darling I am on my way now. How is it all going?'

'Fine sweetheart. The ice buckets are full, the Lilies have bloomed, and the corpses are starting to be rolled in. You'll be fashionably late to arrive if you leave now.'

'I wouldn't have it any other way. See you soon.'

* * * * *

'Excuse me? Hello?'

'Darling, I'm sorry….'

'Christ, what the fuck happened?'

'I'm sorry. I left.'

'Yes. I'm aware. I texted you about sixteen times and no one you work with seemed to know where you had gone either. And Christ, you should have seen Veronica's face when I asked where you were.'

'I'm so sorry.'

'Stop saying sorry and tell me what fucking happened?'

'Are you ok?'

'Am I ok? I'm fine. Except I was left alone in a room full of geriatric, Eastern Suburb millionaires. NOT that I was complaining, but it did look rather odd. Me in my best Vivienne Westwood Kaftan and dripping in Rosary beads and them barely able to stand upright in their pant suits. I assume you're home now, unless you're hiding in that gallery somewhere still?'

'No, I am home. I was probably there briefly while you were. But I came straight home.'

'Well tell me…'

'Veronica and I had an argument.'

'Ah, I see. Well, that makes sense now. In front of anyone?'

'No, I don't think so. Maybe a few people heard but it wasn't a scene.'

'Well I heard and saw nothing if that's any consolation.'

'No, I don't think you were there yet when it started.'

'Tell me. What happened?'

'At about 6:30pm Veronica cornered me in the gallery as I am trying to speak to Ros Packer and excuses herself whilst pulling me to one side. She whispers harshly in my ear that Stephen Radley had arrived, and she would like me to go and greet him and show him around. I try to maintain my composure and tell her that I was busy. She immediately bolts over to Ros Packer and starts pulling her off and then waves me on, apologising audibly to Ros that I had to go and tend to something else.'

'Smooth.'

'I'm kind of in shock for a moment and obviously start to feel instantly anxious, but I think, it's a room full of people, what's he going to try? If anything, if he's pissed enough already, I can just shit talk with him enough to coax him into parting with some more of his hard-inherited cash like the drunk idiot he is. So, I down a drink and then head over to the entrance of the gallery where I find him mostly leaning against a plinth glaring at one of the more graphic of these prints.'

'Which one?'

'Number 39. I can't remember what it's called in Spanish, but it's a scene of the naked bodies of three soldiers all strapped to a tree with various parts of them having been amputated and then impaled onto individual branches. All of them have also had their cocks sliced off.'

'Charming. Unsurprising though that it would appeal to someone like Stephen Radley.'

'So, I approach him and without taking his eyes off the print or acknowledging me, he asks me if I knew if the men in the picture were French or Spanish soldiers.'

'What does it matter?'

'I said as much. Then he turned to me and just smiled but it seemed nervous. Scared even. I noticed his voice was trembling slightly. He asked me then if it was possible to see the print in a different kind of lighting. Possibly in the upstairs space. You know where she has that office and her stockroom?'

'Christ Sake.'

'I didn't care though because again, Veronica was taking people in and out of there all night also. Clients who wanted to see some other artworks she had. So, I knew he wasn't going to be able to get away with trying anything.'

'Right.'

'I tell him that it was fine, I unhook the thing and we go upstairs. I wave to Veronica across the room and gesture that I am taking Radley upstairs and she nods at me but when he turns around, she gives him this awful smile and a thumbs up. He barely even realises who she is.'

'Vile. The both of them.'

'So we are upstairs, alone, and I'm hanging the thing on one of the blank walls and then begin to adjust the light for him and he eventually waddles over to it and bends forward like he was peering in a keyhole just in silence. I say nothing. My heart is pounding though thinking of what exactly he might try given he thinks he's got an in with me now but still just silence while he looks deep into the picture at all the limbs and blood splattered from one side of the frame to the other. Body parts strewn across the foreground and bulging eyes of pain popping out all over. But then he straightens up and heads over to one of the windows looking out in the street and just stares out into it. It was dark but there was a blinding beam of light coming through from one of the street lamps and it pushed his shadow right across to the other side of the room. I asked him if everything was ok, still not moving from where I was standing. But he didn't respond. Then I see, as he turns around slightly that he's fucking crying. Crying, would you believe?'

'Jesus Christ.'

'So, I start to approach him, but he spins right around and sort of just collapses into one of the armchairs and continues to sniff back tears wiping them from his face with both his hands. Saying nothing at all. It was about 5 minutes before I could get him to even look at me. But eventually he raises his head and I see these huge, pathetic, pale blue eyes just glistening with water. And finally, he says, I'm sorry. He starts to sob a little more before he repeats himself, I'm sorry, I'm sorry he keeps saying.'

'Why though?'

'He says, he regretted what happened the other night between us. He said he wasn't sure how it all kind of unfolded and just kept saying he was sorry over and over. I sat down on the chair next to him and just put my arm on his shoulder and tried to tell him it was fine. But he kept interrupting me. He became slightly hysterical about it.'

'I wonder what he thinks happened?'

'I'm lonely, he says. I'm so incredibly lonely.

'Oh.'

'I'm lonely and I'm old, he says. Lonely like you wouldn't believe, like you could never know.'

'That's quite tragic. All that money...'

'I was a bit suspicious for a moment, thinking he was playing some sort of empathy card. Trying to make someone feel sorry enough for him to approach. To hold him. But I just stood there watching and I could see after a moment, it wasn't that. He wasn't being pathetic on purpose. I could tell he hated every second of saying what he was saying. Hated every word of admitting it. Again, this huge, towering figure of the most upper echelon of Sydney high society just a drunken blubbering, lonely mess. Crumpled up on himself. Wet with tears and red with shame. I told him what happened between us wasn't a big deal and to forget it. It didn't bother me. But he just kept saying repeatedly, I'm lonely, I'm old. Finally, after a minute, I could calm him down and start to speak to him normally. Telling him of course he had friends. I knew he did. I had seen him with people all the time. I said I had I assumed he and Veronica were at least close, from what I saw. If not acquaintances. But he dismissed it instantly. Called her a fucking predator would you believe?'

'Yes, I would.'

'Said the only reason he and I ended up together the other night is because of her. She had coaxed him into it. It'd be good for him, she said apparently. To be with a younger guy. Would make him feel alive again. Young. But he said he just felt seedy. Felt even more alone by the end of it. Said he had only ever been with one or two guys before that. He had come to the gallery that night to tell her about not wanting to buy the painting, but then just started to open up to her a bit. Said he was feeling vulnerable and just wanted to chat. She had apparently told him I liked older guys. That I had said to her how handsome he was when he had come in. That I was just waiting for the chance to make a move. And before he knew it, he was sitting in the back of his car with me.'

'Fucking Christ. How did she even know you would though?'

'She didn't. I guess she was backing herself both ways. Desperate, fresh, young, queer employee, keen to make a good impression and an equally desperate, old, lonely client keen to feel some burst of youthful energy. The ideal outcome being tens of thousands of dollars in her pocket.'

'Yuck.'

'It was pathetic really. To watch it all. I felt for a moment, kind of sorry for him. But then it all just turned to blind rage towards her. I told him everything was going to be fine and then he was welcome to talk to me any time if he came in, but I didn't want to become this man's friend. It was sad to see, but I couldn't focus on anything else than getting the fuck out of there. It was stifling me. To have to be burdened with all of this intense sadness of this man I could usually barely stand the sight of. So, I told him to relax upstairs for a moment, pull himself together and then he could leave silently. I would go back downstairs and finish up and then go home as quickly as I could. But as I was hanging the print back on the wall, I see Veronica out of the corner of my eye approaching and I stop. There are still about 10 or so people in the room, mingling about the bar. That was quick, she says smugly and leans in, smiling that fucking ugly, yellow toothed, red wine smile. Next time, she says, you probably won't need to go all the way to Neutral Bay to seal it. She cackles loudly and goes to take a huge gulp of wine, but just before she did, I let go of the print and let it fall heavily onto that concrete floor and it smashes into a thousand pieces. The glass lacerating the paper, crumpling it into a mass of wood and ancient ink. The whole room was instantly silent, and everyone's eyes were on the floor at the car crash I had just caused, except mine. Mine were on Veronica. Her mouth full of the wine she had just taken but not yet swallowed. Her own eyes bulging at the thousands of dollars damage I had just caused her. I let it all sink in. Exactly what I had done without a hit of it being less than wholly intentional. I let it sink right. Next time, I say walking right up to her face and pressing my finger into her sun damaged cleavage, Next time, you can fuck him yourself.'

'Oh honey…'

'And I walk off.

'Well Christ. I guess that is a rather good excuse for leaving early. I only wish I'd hung around now.'

'I imagine she will try and make a thing out of me smashing the thing, and completely ignore the reasoning behind it.'

'And what? Risk being exposed as a fucking trafficker of young boys to seedy old clients of hers in the process? I doubt it. It's $10,000 she is going to have to suck up. You could probably sue her if you wanted to. She'll lose a lot fucking more than an old Goya print in the process. Are you supposed to be working tomorrow?'

'Yes. But I imagine I will go in just to be told to no longer come in. I might just not even go back. I don't even have an employment contract with her and she is still paying me in cash.'

'Well I'm not going to encourage you to throw yourself into a period of poverty darling, but what is it worth for your mental health? And plenty of other dealers around will be chomping at the bit to get you in their galleries. Better ones.'

'Do I even want that anymore though?'

'What do you mean?'

'I don't know.'

'You wanted this ever since I met you though, to work in galleries. I think it's just a bit of a false start. She hasn't been a good introduction I don't think. In actual fact she's been a fucking awful introduction.'

'She runs the most successful private gallery in the entire city. Where do I go from here?'

'You don't need to be with her for that reason.'

'I've seen a lot of this world, this fucking art world. Of Sydney and its money and its big houses and beaches. All in less than a year. I don't think I was ready for what was behind the curtain. What happens if I don't want to do it anymore?'

'For work?'

'Work. Anything.'

'I don't know darling. I don't have an answer for that, I'm sorry.'

'I think I am feeling rather tired of it all this evening. I may sleep for a few days now.'

'I understand my love. And nothing from James still?'

'Nothing.'

'Hmmm…'

'I think that's it darling. I think he's moved on or away from it all. I didn't see him at the pool yesterday or today either.'

'It's only been a few days though. Don't be too hard on yourself.'

'I know it's absurd isn't it?'

'It is, but you can't help it.'

'Anyway, when is Darren coming over?

'In the next 30 mins or so. Apparently.'

'Not so sure now?'

'No no, he's been texting, but y'know whether or not he shows up…'

'I really do hope that he's taken a minute to look at his behaviour on the weekend. I know he most likely hasn't though.'

'I think he has. I feel an apology coming on.'

'I hope so.'

'Get some rest darling and we can chat later.'

WEDNESDAY

'Sweetheart how is your ear now? Did they rebandage it before you left?'

'Fine. They said it will heal ok.'

'Did they redress it?'

'Yes. I took a look at it in a mirror as well before they did it up again. I thought the earring might have split the lobe in two but it's ok. I think when he punched it, it's just knocked it out, not torn it.'

'And your nose?'

'Still swollen but apparently not broken.'

'That's surprising.'

'Doesn't seem to be as strong as he presents.'

'Or you are stronger than you present.'

'Or that.'

'What time did you get home from the hospital?'

'Maybe 2am? I just got a taxi.'

'I really should have taken you home.'

'I was fine my love honestly. You did more than enough.'

'Any messages from him?'

'No.'

'Nothing online?'

'Nothing.'

'Ok.

'What will happen now? Will the police go find him?'

'I doubt it.'

'What the fuck, why not?'

'They came in after I had been bandaged up the first time by the nurses, probably about 30 mins after you left. Two of them. Men. Neither of them even sat down when they were talking to me which I knew meant they weren't interested at all in this taking any longer than it needed to.'

'What did they ask?'

'Well they started asking about the actual incident first. Like where it happened, if I thought anyone might have seen it. I told them everything I remembered. The carpark where we were. Obviously, what he looks like. About where he told me lived, about what he told me he did for a living. This dark blue Nike hoodie he was hearing, his black jeans. What that ridiculous car he drives looks like. But I couldn't tell them anything useful like what his license plate was. All I have is his phone number, a short stream of very basic text messages and a name. A fucking name that I don't even know is real.'

'Darling don't get yourself too worked up just try and relax, we don't have to talk about it if you want to rest.'

'No, it's fine. I'm ok. They asked me if I had a picture of him which of course I don't but I told him that we had been to ARQ a few times together and they would have CCTV footage of him. I thought this was quite a good idea actually but the minute I mentioned ARQ, they both shot a look at one another that was more subtle than a smirk, but it wasn't far from it. Just a sort of grimace at the mention of it and then the realisation of what they were actually dealing with. One of them even put away their fucking notepad. But I carried on.'

'Ok.'

'Then of course the one still taking notes asks how we knew each other.'

'Hmmm.'

'I was honest, I told them everything. About Manhunt, about Bodyline and then finally about his episode in the club. I told them that he had messaged me that night to meet up, but hadn't made any plans, so I had assumed he had just wanted to talk about it. About that moment. Maybe even apologise to me for causing a scene and then talk about it a bit more. But when he had texted to say he was here but wasn't interested in coming inside my apartment I sort of got the impression something was off. I went anyway. I got into his car and he was sitting there with his hood up. He still had a smouldering cigarette in the ashtray. His knee was bouncing up and down erratically so I could tell he was nervous, but he was always nervous when we met. He was always poised like he was about to bolt off in the opposite direction at any minute, so I didn't think anything of it. I couldn't quite see his face from the darkness of the car and his hood, and he was appearing like he was trying to obscure it as much as possible. For a moment it was just silence while we both stared out into the darkness of that street. The only light coming from the glow of the buttons on his dashboard. Then he finally speaks…'

'Ok.'

'You raped me on Sunday night, he says.'

'I'm sorry what?'

'He says it again. You raped me, on Sunday night. And before I could even think how to respond, he turns to finally make eye contact and says, You took me home when I was drunk, you put me to sleep in your bed and then raped me while I was passed out. You fucking raped me.'

'Holy shit…'

'I just sat there, sunken right back into the car seat and looked at him. I could see his eyes now and they were wet but not with tears of being upset. I could see already it was total rage and I began to get concerned. But I wasn't going to sit there and be accused of rape without at least trying to defend myself. So, I just very calmly said that it wasn't true and asked him how he could think that.'

'And what did he say.'

'He said when he woke up the next morning, he could feel it. That he had been fucked. He said there was even still lube there. And he was in pain.'

'God…'

'But it's not true!'

'Darling, I believe you.'

'It's not true. We didn't do anything. Let alone that. He was so fucking drunk he could barely stand up. What interest would I have in fucking around with a totally comatose man?'

'I believe you.'

'But then I started second guessing myself. Like trying to think back, whilst I am defending myself. Did we have sex? Could we have, and I just cannot remember, in some drunken haze? But darling, you know me. I have probably topped maybe twice, three times max in my life. Why would I have thought to start then and there and like that?'

'Darling it's not true.'

'But I cannot remember anything at all.'

'It's because it didn't happen. You're trying to remember something that didn't happen, it doesn't mean you have forgotten it.'

'He kept going on about how he knew immediately what had happened the minute he woke up. How much pain he was in. And I just kept trying to speak but to suggest he might have dreamt it or something, anything, that it wasn't true, and I never would.'

'When did it turn?'

'I must have started to raise my voice or something to try and let myself be heard over his constant interrupting and I think it just triggered him and before I even knew it, I was holding my face with my hands to try and shield myself from his fists, just blow after blow smashing into me. I managed to somehow fumble my way to the door handle and sort of fell out of the car onto the gravel. He must have connected a few times because when I pulled my hands away, a pool of blood had formed in my palms and was still steaming from my mouth as I was gazing down into it. I was so dizzy and in such shock I couldn't even steady myself to stand before he had managed to get out of the car and continue beating me whilst I lay on the ground. He knelt down initially and continued to punch me. I could tell he was using both his arms, like a boxer. I could tell he had done this before or had trained to do this. He was too precise and calculated. It wasn't like the way people punch to escape or defend themselves. It was punching to inflict harm. He seemed to tire after a moment and stood up. I was completely curled up by this stage like a fucking armadillo on that filthy ground. My mouth was now almost entirely full of blood and that overpowering taste of metal was seeping down my throat and I wanted to cough but I couldn't. I could barely breathe.

I thought he might have been done. Tired himself out when there was a pause. I could hear him taking a few steps back, crunching the gravel under his shoes. I started to uncurl myself thinking I might be able to make a run for it, but then the toe of his shoe came powering into my back like a battering ram and completely incapacitated me. I couldn't even hold myself in my pathetic ball anymore. I just lay there, splayed out, winded, bloodied, wheezing for air and trying to clear my throat of my own blood.'

'And not a single person around to try and help? Fucking cunts of this city…'

'He must have gotten tired of it or just had enough because he stopped and went to walk away, but obviously needed one final shot at the title. I heard his footsteps stop just before he went back around to the driver's side. He comes back to where I am laying and kneels down before gargling up a huge ball of phlegm and spitting towards my face. I try and wipe it off, but it just blends in with the blood around my mouth and eyes. I get the impression that not only is he just watching me writhe and struggle, but that he's smirking, smiling even whilst he does.

Eventually I hear him stand up again again and in a deep, sinister growl he says inches from my face, You disgusting, fucking queen he says. You, fucking nasty queer.'

'Jesus…'

'And then he fires up that car and disappears into the darkness.'

'How long were you laying there?'

'Not long. I got up and ran, as best I could with not an ounce of air in my lungs left from his fucking boot, but I ran, or some chaotic form of running, to any place I thought there might be people. And even as I was wandering through those poorly light streets, blood pouring out of me, barely able to stand straight I was thinking, How? How has he come up with this idea? What could have possibly happened in this vague moment of our lives that this man, this beast, seems to think he has been assaulted? By me of all fucking people. Then it hit me.'

'Ok.'

'It must have been when he went to the fucking sauna. It has to be…'

'Bodyline? When?'

'That night. After I told him to go and calm down outside and he disappeared for a few hours. Remember I told you he came back smelling of chlorine?'

'Yes, I remember.'

'He would have gone into Bodyline.'

'And you think something happened?'

'It must have. He was obviously too fucked to remember. It didn't strike me when I saw him that anything sinister had happened to him. He just looked drunk.'

'So, he's gone into Bodyline whilst you were watching the drag show and done something with a guy, consensual or not consensual, and then woke up the next day aware something's happened and found himself in bed with you.'

'I believe so.'

'Honey that's… I don't quite know what to say.'

'I was in the middle of telling the cops what had happened, and it just sort of dawned on me.'

'How did you tell them then?'

'I stopped. I said nothing.'

'Why not?'

'I can't darling.'

'You have to sweetheart.'

'How in the hell are they going to be able to process that when they could barely grasp that fact we met on an internet chatroom called fucking ManHunt? You do realise that Gay Panic is still a legal defence to assault and even murder in this fucking state?'

'He can't.'

'He can. So, I said nothing. I sat there and said it was nothing more than a lover's tiff. I sat there and made it out like it was just two guys who got into a heated argument and I came out worse off. Bruised and beaten but not broken. I sat there and said it was nothing. Nothing for them to do. Nothing for them to follow up. And that was the end of it.'

'Oh darling…'

'They seemed satisfied.'

'I bet they did. Because you saved them the embarrassment of having to engage with this world any further. You saved them a trip to a gay sauna and a gay club. But at what cost?'

'I don't have the strength to see this through. I just want to be left alone and forget about it. Don't be angry on my behalf. I can't bear it.'

'I'm sorry my love. No one wants that. You take this as far as you feel like you can. It's cold comfort to you now I know, but I promise you, he will get what he deserves eventually.'

'Well he's just a ghost now.'

'He appears to have always been one though, doesn't he?'

'Vaporized back into the chaos of the city once again.'

'Try to get some rest my love and I will pop round to check on you a bit later this evening.'

'Ok. I love you.'

'I love you too.'

THURSDAY

'I just got back from your campus darling. Everything is settled now for you to take your classes from home this week, they said. They want you to check in again next week and see how you're feeling.'

'Thank you, my love. Did they ask for much more information?'

'No. I think they seemed to understand the severity by what I had already said. I wouldn't have told them much more anyway. They don't need to know. They were very kind.'

'Angels. The lot of you.'

'Have you been able to get much done today?'

'Just some reading. It's been a nice distraction actually. Dr Huxley emailed me some articles to look at and the slides from his lecture today. It was about Absinthe and art in the 19th Century.'

'Fucking Huxley. Honestly.'

'It was interesting actually. He was asking us to compare it to the use of LSD in the 60's.'

'I imagine he's quite the authority on both. Poor thing. Is he still wearing those sand coloured, corduroy suits?'

'Yes. And quite proudly too. It's very much the uniform of the Professor of Art History I feel. An ill-fitting, slightly soiled, pale suit, oily hair, rosacea and thick, black circular glasses. He's sweet though. I feel like he'd be great dinner table company. Maybe we should invite him over one night. For one of my famous dinners. Strangely I feel he'd be one of the more reserved guests if he were to join.'

'Absinthe, LSD and your cooking would be a catastrophic combination.'

'The drugs to simply numb the senses and the food to line the stomach.'

'Of course.'

'I'd kill for either of the two right now.'

'I understand why, but probably not the best time to be doing it.'

'A minor dulling of the senses darling is all I think I need now. Just enough to allow a scratching of the surface into that layer of all those strange and wonderful areas of my mind that all the mayhem with day to day, tries to silence.'

'I think Dr Huxley is a fine example of someone who may have tapped in a little too far though and can't find his way out again.'

'Well he's not an artist, is he? He's an academic. He probably has tapped too far but there was no need for him to go in there in the first place. Artist's need to operate on that level of existence that is just slightly above or below where everyone else is. To see something in a different way and then present back to us to try and understand as mortals who cannot or choose not to go there…'

'I think good art might have existed before Absinthe. And well before LSD. Isn't it all just an excuse for people who are too lazy to take the time to learn how to tap into that part of their brain, in a sober way?'

'No. It's not laziness, it's a conscious relinquishing of control. It's you saying to yourself, here is the world, he is my world, I say when I wake up, I say when I eat, when I move, when I fuck. But here is this little pill/drink/pipe that is going to steer the boat for a little while and I am just going to sit back and watch the scenery. See what my world looks like when I am in the backseat. And it's in those moments you see beauty where there was none before. Take what Dr. Huxley is saying in this lecture when he mentions Toulouse-Lautrec for instance. These cabaret houses were where the lowest of the lows could be found. Dandy's, prostitutes, alcoholics, opium addicts.

People to be considered barely functioning on the fringes of civil society, huddled together in this hot, hazy saloon full of tits and syphilis. And they existed well before he visited them. Well before. But what artist was able to see their beauty until him? What artist was willing to sit there and absorb anything about it all beyond what was there on the surface. What was once pure filth was now suddenly beautiful and erotic.'

'You think Absinthe did all that?'

'I think it certainly helped. Yes.'

'Right. Well how are you feeling today?'

'Physically you mean?'

'Let's start with that.'

'Fine. Swollen. Both eyes are black now and appear to be turning blacker as the day goes one. But nothing a good paint job with some heavy foundation and a bronzer can't fix.'

'That a girl.'

'I took the bandages off my ear this morning. I think it's fine now and my nose seems to have not swollen much more. All in all, it's ok considering.'

'And your head?'

'It's fine darling I feel ok.'

'That's good. And I imagine you haven't heard from him?'

'No, his profile is gone. Deleted. Blocked or whatever. Everything is gone.'

'Ok. And do you feel safe staying there considering he knows where you live?'

'Weirdly yes. I can't really explain why, but I am oddly confident he won't return. I think if he really wanted to, he could have done more.'

'I actually don't want to think about it.'

'Deep down I think he knew it wasn't me. That I wasn't responsible for whatever happened to him that night. But I think in at that moment in the carpark I was, for him, everything he hated, everything he was terrified of and didn't understand, about being queer. All the outward sexual expression, the femininity, drag, all of it. And he wanted it to go away. To be pushed down into the dirt and buried so he could run away and forget any of it happened.'

'It will catch up with him, I promise. Even if the cops decide not to do anything about it. It will.'

'You know what else? I was sitting in my garden just before and I heard this car slow down outside my house. I couldn't see it, but it sounded just like his. This low, very heavy drone. Like the heavy bass of a large sound system. And an engine that rattled like marbles in a can. And for a split second I thought he was sat there. Idling outside my bedroom window waiting.'

'This is what I was worried about.'

'But my reaction wasn't to hide, or to call you or the police or anything. It was something along the lines of excitement. I was excited to see him. I was sitting there and in the pit of my stomach it was the feeling I would get when I saw him appear out of nowhere in the dark at ARQ or when a message from him would randomly show up online. How have I already seemed to have forgotten what happened or even forgiven him?'

'You had fallen for this man darling. For whatever reason. You were seeing him with only love in your eyes and you were looking for all the things to justify that. But that also means you were probably disregarding all the things telling you this wasn't someone you should be feeling this way about. All the little signs. Being in love is like being drunk. You have no time for comprehending important details.'

'I won't seek him out. I don't want to see him. But I say that now. What if I come across him outside at some point in the street and my first reaction is to just smile and hug him because that's what I would do normally? To just have some innocuous conversation about how he's been and then start flirting with him? Start touching him on the arm as we talk. Start laughing at the stupid things he's saying. I am not scared of him. Of what he might do to me again. I am strong. I can take a beating. Bruises disappear and cuts heal. But what if he sees this person he's beaten and left to bleed out in a carpark, is fine. This person he tried to mutilate, is functioning and is even still fucking infatuated with him and he realises he can do it all again. And it's fine. That is what I am scared of.'

'I understand darling. I think you are just going to have to spend a lot of time processing this and just prepare yourself as best you can to respond in the way you want to you, should you see him, not the way you think he wants you to.'

'I will.'

'Do you need me to do anything more with your Uni work? Do you need me to collect any papers or

whatever for you? I'll be passing that way later today
on my way to the pool.'

'No, my love. You've done more than enough, thank
you.'

* * * * *

'What do you think of this?'

'What?'

'One second, the picture is coming....'

'Oh wow.'

'Yes, I started with a bit of concealer to cover the
black eyes and y'know what? I just thought fuck it.
Keep going. Who knew I'd make such a gorgeous
Queen? Such a gorgeous Nasty Queer. It's my Fuck
You to him, I thought. These eyelashes and this
contouring. This lipstick. This blush. The eye shadow.
The glitter. All of it.'

'You're beautiful. I love it.'

'I may have polished off a bottle of wine also whilst
doing it too.'

'Impressive even more so then my dear.'

'How was your swim?'

'Fine.'

'And nothing?'

'For what?'

'No sign of James?'

'No.'

'I'm sorry darling. I don't really know what to say about it. It still really is rather early days though isn't it?'

'No, he's gone. It's done.'

'What do you mean?'

'I went to his house…'

'Oh fuck.'

'He's gone.'

'What do you mean you went to his fucking house? Like unannounced?'

'Sort of.'

'Are you insane?'

'For months he had made himself just appear every fucking single time I was at the pool. Every day I would see him. No matter what time I would be there, he would always just be getting into the pool as I would be. Our schedules were entirely in sync. So, he could follow me into the change room. So, he could follow me out. Watch me. Maybe talk to me. But every fucking time, he was there. And equally as effectively, he has managed to disappear.'

'Ok.'

'I just wanted to see him. I didn't even need to speak to him. It was just this burning desire to convince myself that I hadn't completely made up the experience of being with him on the weekend. That it wasn't a fucking dream. I just wanted to see him and know it was all real. So, I left the pool and went to the little bar we had drinks at and just sat there, my hair still wet from swimming all afternoon. I even ordered a small glass of that same wine we drank together. I just sat there, glaring out into the street and across at his house through those same dusty windows, waiting for some sort of sign that there was life in there. Any life.'

'Oh, my love. It's such a sad picture.'

'I didn't mean for it to be. I just needed some sort of closure and I am not even sure what that was going to look like. Maybe he would have noticed me. Maybe he would have come across and just told me he couldn't see me anymore. I would have been fine with that, I think. Just to say, listen we can't talk anymore, let's just go back to what it was. I didn't mean for it to escalate. I would have been ok I think.'

'I get that.'

'The girl behind the bar came over and when she took my glass, she seemed to recognise me and asked me where my friend was. I just smiled and looked away, because I had no idea how to respond to it. But just as she was about to leave, I turned and asked her if he came in often. My friend. She paused for a minute and sort of looked confused and just said that it was the first time she had ever seen either of us there.'

'Ok.'

'I just stood up and found myself walking slowly towards his front door. I just wanted to see him. It's all I wanted. Just to look at him, I didn't need to say anything. Or to hear him say anything to me.'

'Oh sweetheart…'

'And suddenly I was there. Staring at his front door. In my shorts and sandals. Wet and sad. Pressing his doorbell. I had no idea what I was going to say. I had no idea what to do if it wasn't him who answered. I didn't have a plan. It was just a sort of numbing moment of insanity.'

'Maybe the wine also?'

'As soon as I pressed the doorbell a light went on at the ground level and I heard some movement. I think it was only then I snapped into the realisation of what I had done. But even then, if I had turned to run away, whoever answered would have seen me. He might have seen me running off down the street and the whole thing would be fucking pointless. I had to stay. And so finally the door creaked open slowly and this older woman appeared. Short, very dark features with thick glasses and wearing this sort of stained apron. She smiled at me warmly as she said, Hello. I mumbled something completely incomprehensible first and she leaned in forward and I realised she clearly hadn't understood. So, I just cleared my throat and said, Would James be home at all?'

'I imagine this is not the wife?'

'Well I didn't know and didn't want to make any assumptions. I had quickly concocted some ridiculous story that I was a friend of his from the pool and that he had left something there that I was returning.'

'Well done.'

'But as I asked her, she just stood there sort of creasing her eyebrows togethers looking more and more confused. Who, she finally said. James, I repeated, Is James home? She shook her head and smiled again politely and said, No one lives here darling. The house had been on the market for over a year now. She said she was the cleaner from the estate agent. The owner, she knew, lived overseas but was a woman named Cynthia. Not a man named James.'

'Shit…'

'And that was it. I thanked her, smiled and walked off.'

'I'm sorry.'

'I don't know where he is. I don't know anything more…'

'What do you think is the truth?'

'Nothing. I don't think anything now. I don't know anything about him. Whatever happened in that moment was all it was ever going to be. These men are ghosts. Darren, James. They don't exist.'

'Well they do, just not in our dimension. Just not on a plane of existence that we can hold and see them.'

'He's dipped into my life and then just disappeared into a beautiful nothingness again.'

'I'm sorry darling, truly.'

'There's nothing to be sorry for or about my love. I should have been more aware. I should have noticed more things that would have made this more obvious.'

'How? You were falling for him. You just told me we ignore details like drunkards, whilst we are in love.'

'I know.'

'And it's our god given fucking right to be seduced by love. Why should we look at details? Why should we be lucid and rational in love? Because there are fucking men out there who play with our hearts like this?'

'I worry that these moments chip away at the core of my vulnerability. That there is such a finite supply of this wholesome affection that I can give to someone and that all it takes is a few moments like this. Of being raw and open, of allowing myself to feel, like truly feel what infatuation and lust is, but then having that shot down. Blocked or just ignored and forgotten. Before it's not possible anymore. Before the well is dry.'

'I hope not.'

'Me either.'

'What can I do? What do you need me to do? I want to help. Or do you want to be alone?'

'I don't quite know.'

'Shall I come over? I will bring more wine. I think I have a bottle left somewhere. C'mon, let's just sit and chat. I can cook even. I am all dolled up as well.'

'No, I think I want to go out.'

'Out?'

'Yes.'

'Amazing. Lets. Where though?'

'Let's go to the Rugby game.'

'What? With your family?''

'Yes. Let's go to that.'

'I, ah…

Are you sure?'

'Yes, let's get really fucking hammered on cheap
wine and go.'

'Ok.'

'Let's go and laugh at all the fucking ridiculous things
straight people do at these games. Let's go scream
with them when the players call each other faggots.
Let's shout along with them to the lyrics of all those
queer songs they long like Rocket Man or Don't Stop
Me Now when they blast it over the speakers. Let's
squeal and point at the giant screens when they show
the inside of the changing rooms; the players' chests
and bulges inside their short shorts. Let's go and just
be really fucking gay.'

'Darling I'm drunk and am in full drag makeup.'

'Perfect.'

'And what are we to say to your family, when asked about all this?'

'About what?'

'About everything that's happened.'

'We smile, and nod along politely and say absolutely nothing at all.'

Printed in Great Britain
by Amazon

56380413R00130